C000162773

G R JORDAN

The First Minister

A Highlands and Islands Detective Thriller

First edition

ISBN: 978-1-915562-39-5

This book was professionally typeset on Reedsy.
Find out more at reedsy.com

Do not brood over your past mistakes and failures as this will only fill your mind with grief, regret and depression. Do not repeat them in the future.

SWAMI SIVANANDA

Contents

Foreword

The events of this book, while based around real locations in the north of Scotland, are entirely fictional and all characters do not represent any living or deceased person. All companies are fictitious representations.

Acknowledgement

To Ken, Jean, Colin, Evelyn, John and Rosemary for your work in bringing this novel to completion, your time and effort is deeply appreciated.

Novels by G R Jordan

The Highlands and Islands Detective series (Crime)

1. Water's Edge
2. The Bothy
3. The Horror Weekend
4. The Small Ferry
5. Dead at Third Man
6. The Pirate Club
7. A Personal Agenda
8. A Just Punishment
9. The Numerous Deaths of Santa Claus
10. Our Gated Community
11. The Satchel
12. Culhwch Alpha
13. Fair Market Value
14. The Coach Bomber
15. The Culling at Singing Sands
16. Where Justice Fails
17. The Cortado Club
18. Cleared to Die
19. Man Overboard!
20. Antisocial Behaviour
21. Rogues' Gallery
22. The Death of Macleod - Inferno Book 1

Kirsten Stewart Thrillers (Thriller)

The Contessa Munroe Mysteries (Cozy Mystery)

The Patrick Smythe Series (Crime)

1. The Disappearance of Russell Hadleigh
2. The Graves of Calgary Bay
3. The Fairy Pools Gathering

Austerley & Kirkgordon Series (Fantasy)

1. Crescendo!
2. The Darkness at Dillingham
3. Dagon's Revenge
4. Ship of Doom

Supernatural and Elder Threat Assessment Agency (SETAA) Series (Fantasy)

1. Scarlett O'Meara: Beastmaster

Island Adventures Series (Cosy Fantasy Adventure)

1. Surface Tensions

Dark Wen Series (Horror Fantasy)

1. The Blasphemous Welcome
2. The Demon's Chalice

Chapter 01

It wasn't that the armchair was uncomfortable; it was the fact that he sat in it every day. The view wasn't unpalatable either, but the same view every day for the last year had become, frankly, boring. Yes, some days the mist swept through. Other days, there was that dreich drizzle, the almost mundane scourge of Hebridean life. You expected cool and wet weather. In summer, there were a few days that were quite glorious, including one which forced him to move his chair for the sun had broken through in and blazed upon him. Instead of his usual jumper and shirt, he'd been down to the thinnest fabric shirt he had. His lips smiled thinly remembering it because it was a different day. It was a day that broke the routine of the norm.

Yet he was thankful, for not everyone got the care and attention that he did. The women that worked in the care home were friendly, a bit heavy-handed and maybe a little loose with their talk. He had heard one the previous day discussing a women's night out before a wedding. He was calmly ignoring it, instead reading a commentary on Job. When she spoke about the inflatable thing and how they were cavorting on it with their drinks, he felt distinctly uncomfortable and even offended. There was no place for talk like that. Not in the workplace.

In his years as a police officer, he never would've spoken like that. Yes, at times, he had to speak in a firm, confrontational way, but never with such rudeness or such a lack of propriety. As a church elder, he'd overseen many generations of ministers. He'd helped many of them become better preachers, better examples for the community. He had advised them on their wives' place, to not let them get above their station.

Then he'd had the stroke, and nowadays he needed help just to go to the bathroom. He wasn't totally infirm, not completely restricted. Three times a day he got up to walk. He made it down that corridor and back. Each painting was the same as the day he'd come in here. Each painting showed nothing new when you looked at them. Maybe if they had that Dutch guy, Van Gok or whatever it was he was called. Although he'd never understood what the excitement was about those flowers.

It would've been better if they had some historical photographs, places he could reminisce about. His life now was stuck in this one building in Leverburgh at the south end of Harris. He'd worked up in Stornoway before moving further down. Then he had tended his crop for five years before the stroke hit him. Now the house had been sold, the money being used to fund this rather drab life.

It was a sin to not be content. A sin to question what the Lord was doing, but recently, Angus McNeil had more than enough reason to question Him.

'Hello, Angus. How are we today? How's the view?'

There came a chortle from the young woman that passed him by. Sarah was a young mother of three. Angus knew this because she told him about twice a week. She'd moved up here with her husband looking for an idyllic lifestyle and had found a job in the care home. She had tattoos down one arm. Colourful, but it was wrong. Your body was perfect, given by the Lord. You didn't mark it like that.

The care staff had light green tops; polo shirts presumably supplied by the care home. Some of Angus's money they were wearing. They looked smart, in fairness, but the staff could wear whatever they wanted below these polo tops. A few of the older ladies had large skirts that drifted around just above the ankle. Sensible, appropriate. But Sarah wore jeans. They were often tight and blue, and she tucked the green top in so tight that Angus couldn't help but notice her figure. She was also red of hair, and for some reason, had a ring that went through her eyebrow. Angus didn't get this jewellery fascination. Earrings he could handle, but not the way they did it these days.

'You look like a pygmy.' His one comment on the matter.

That wouldn't be allowed today either, would it? You couldn't call people pygmies. It'd have to be indigenous, something or other. The world was spinning too fast for him, and he didn't like becoming old. He didn't like the fact that he was no longer in control, no longer had a say. Some days, they even had to wipe his backside; the indignity of it.

He watched as Sarah crossed the room, bent over to make some tea, and then brought him a large cup. It was milky, always too milky; and never warm enough. He'd questioned Sarah about this before and she said it was because he threw it around himself. She didn't want him scalded.

He took the cup from her and then watched as she turned to make more. He found his eyes following her and then shouted at himself. A woman who'd become so brazen was not one for his eyes to follow. He felt the anger bubbling up. Why was he

3

here? Lord, why was he here?

'Oh, I nearly forgot, Angus,' said Sarah. 'Got a letter for you. Are you okay with it?'

'Of course, I'll be okay, dear,' he said. 'Have you ever thought about skirts?'

'Oh, you don't wear them, not with the kids. I mean, I've got a long summer one for when it's boiling, but it hasn't got that hot here, has it? But jeans are more practical, do you not think?'

She turned almost as if she was modelling, raising half her backside towards him, and Angus shook his head. But he didn't look away. He found himself unable to look away. He was stronger when he was younger, more determined.

'You going to open it, then?' asked Sarah.

'I will. I'll do it now. You can continue making the tea.'

She would not get to see what was being delivered. This was private. You didn't examine other people's letters. No doubt she'd say she was just there to help, make sure he could open it.

He pulled hard. At least he thought it was hard, trying to rip the envelope apart, but it didn't work. Then her face was there, smiling down at him as her hands removed the envelope from his and opened it with one quick movement, her nail slipping along the top edge.

'There you go, love. Is that okay?'

He grunted, but watched her as she turned away. He used to be strong. Someone like that never would've entertained him. Never would've brought thoughts to mind that shouldn't be there, but Sarah did every day.

Why won't you take me away from here, Lord? he thought.

He fumbled with the pages, dropping one on the floor, and

Sarah brought it back to him. The stroke had really messed him up. Angus used to be coordinated. He used to work out on the croft, tending sheep, planting vegetables, cutting peats in the summer. He was a powerful man, a proud man. Maybe he'd been too proud, and this was God punishing him.

He settled down with the letter and began to read. It was addressed to him, but there was no address at the top of the letter, so he couldn't see who it had come from. Slowly he read it, and then he stopped. The sickness of it. How could someone write this? How could someone… His tea was sitting on the edge of the chair and it fell as he trembled at the acts described.

Sarah was over in a shot. The tea had fortunately gone to one side, but Angus was clearly affected.

'Are you okay?' asked Sarah. 'Angus, are you okay? Is there pain? Can you feel any pain?'

He gave a slight shake of his head, the letter still lying on his lap, one hand vaguely holding onto it.

'Is it the letter?'

He nodded. Slowly. He didn't look back at it. He didn't need to see that letter. Sarah took it off him. She began to read. She shouldn't be doing that, but Angus couldn't stop her.

'The dirty bastards,' said Sarah. 'What the hell's this? Do you know the people who wrote you this?'

Angus sat there, his face reddening.

'It's like some sort of porn thing, isn't it? It's like some sort of… Blimey!'

Sarah wasn't disgusted. She was almost laughing, but Angus felt he was violated. He never agreed with that sort of thing anyway, but these days, well, men could be with men. *It was still wrong, though. Still wrong in the eyes of the Lord*, he thought.

5

Some of the church had changed. Some of the church had fallen asunder. Had the Lord changed? But this wasn't two men being together. This was abusive. One man abusing the other. The detail. The detail....

'Flipping heck,' said Sarah. 'I don't think we should be reading this. It gets a bit sick towards the end, doesn't it?'

It got sick at the start, thought Angus. *Was sick the whole way through.*

'I'm going to report this,' said Sarah. 'I'm going to report it to the police. You shouldn't be receiving stuff like this. There's no name at the end of it either. There's no address. Did you ever get letters like this before, Angus? Ever?'

He shook his head slowly. *Why are you punishing me?* He said to himself. *Why, God? Why do I get this at my time of life?* He sat in the silence, awaiting an answer.

* * *

'Reverend Barkley, if you could just stand over to the side there, we'll be live in two minutes.'

The Reverend Hugh Barkley nodded and obediently stepped over onto the path that ran alongside the ruined church behind him. He hadn't wanted to do this, preferring a quieter life, but he oversaw the parish. The TV crew had come, and his parishioners wouldn't understand why he didn't want himself up in the public forum.

He'd managed a quiet life since those days. He'd squirrelled away, but now he was doing a live broadcast interview. The woman who guided them over was quite the celebrity on Scottish TV. Some twenty years his junior, but she looked extremely professional. Smart, with long grey trousers and matching jacket, brown hair immaculately held in place.

He felt he had too much makeup on. Was it blusher? Something like that. They were constantly wiping around his face. People had said the television made you look fatter, and looking at the woman about to interview him, he thought that might be true. She looked incredibly slim, and yet on the television you thought she could do with a losing a bit. TV was funny.

The day was warm but a little windy. Standing in his dog collar, black trousers, and black suit jacket, Hugh remembered a time when there was more colour in his life. It was long ago, but not forgotten.

'One minute,' said the woman beside him. 'Are you good?'

'Yes, I am,' said Hugh. 'It's okay. I know my stuff.'

'I'll keep it simple. The questions will just be what we've asked before.'

'Okay,' said Hugh.

He watched her turn away to talk to someone, and he thought of a time when he really would've enjoyed this. Back in those days, he was up for anything, but it had been a long and distinguished career within the church. He had said nothing controversial. Done nothing controversial. He'd simply chugged along, often helping people. He kept his appetites in check.

After all, he was to set a good example. Though he could count the number of men and women interesting him, but everything was kept in the mind. That was the thing, wasn't it? If it was in the mind, nobody else could see it. The mind was the place for it. It did no damage. And it could still be remarkably enjoyable.

'We are live in five, four, three, two, one, go.'

Hugh stood, smiling as bright as an excited lemon. Beside him, Scotland's finest outdoor reporter talked of the church building behind them. There had been a restoration fund and visitors were now going to come and look at the building. That was it, though, wasn't it? All these buildings being restored to come and be looked at, not to be used.

Hugh found that strange even though he wasn't really that committed to the God behind the church. Still, he couldn't complain. As a boss, he hadn't been tough. He had let him live out life in anonymity. If he'd been a hard boss, he would have been pulled out to pay for his sins, but no. He'd be all right for the next twenty years. He enjoyed his beef on a Sunday after a few inspirational words, and then back to watching the world go around.

Hugh became suddenly aware that he was being asked a question, something about the fundraising, and he blurted his prepared speech.

'Really, it's been a team effort. They've all pulled together so well. We fundraised both online and through various other collections.'

There were some people behind the interviewer. Beyond her blonde hair, he could see four figures in black coming towards him. They were masked.

'It's not often you get a parish coming together so well and rarely that you... Who the hell are they?'

The interviewer turned because the four figures were almost upon them. She shouted, but was picked up by one and thrown to the side. A smaller black figure stepped forward and Hugh saw the knife before it was driven hard into his shoulder. He screamed.

One of the crew ran forward, and Hugh could hear them

being pummelled back. Suddenly, his hands were being tied behind his back, which made the pain from the knife wound even stronger. It was bleeding. He was sure it was bleeding, although it was hard to tell because of the darkness of his jacket.

His legs were suddenly tied, and then two of the men in black were carrying him away. The smaller figure was still wielding a knife around, but there only was the interviewer, a cameraman, a soundman and a lighting engineer. They were being kept at a distance.

'Phone the police,' shouted Hugh, and then was hit in the face.

It was sore, as it wasn't a tap. It was a full-blown smack. Why were they after him? It was a church. It was just a church being restored. He heard a van door being opened, and he was flung, dropping a couple of feet onto the floor of the van. One of his fingers went down, pointing straight, and jabbed back inside of him. He couldn't reach the sore finger being behind him, and when he tried to roll, the van started up and drove away. Instead of rolling himself into an upright position, he tumbled backwards, his head cracking off the side of the van. The blackness inside of the vehicle became a new blackness inside of the mind.

Chapter 02

Macleod stood up behind his desk and smiled at the bunch of papers sitting on the right-hand side in the rather neatly labelled paper tray. He was getting the hang of this, all the documentation, all the bureaucracy he had to do, and the system he needed to maintain it. The secretary was new, but she'd been the breath of fresh air he'd required. He swore she looked at him like some sort of dilapidated grandpa. She was only twenty-three, but she was a bundle of energy and had swept through the office organising things.

It was like Ross had got a daughter. She did what a secretary was there to do, tidy it all up and present the major things that the boss needed to do, while taking away the minutiae and the nonsense. She could even make coffee. He hoped he wasn't being rude to the younger generation because he generally found they were rubbish at it. Yet Lorraine could make a fantastic coffee.

What he liked most was the fact that he could go out for lunch with Jane most days unless there was a particular case he had to investigate. Jane had revelled in this idea, and she believed now he was a DCI, he seemed to control time better than when he was the DI on a case.

Hope was becoming much more adept at her new role as well. He understood she differed from him. Her strengths lay in different places, but he'd let her get on with it, always with a watchful eye. After all, it was his job, and he was her friend. Friends didn't let friends get into difficulty.

The team was fine, although Macleod had other responsibilities beyond them. He covered off a few other departments and took his time away from the murder team directly. However, he was always available to step back in if the case demanded it. Thankfully, it hadn't.

The investigation at the golf club had gone smoothly enough. They'd got there, Hope had got there, and she was well backed up, for Clarissa was more than just a sergeant. She was savvy, an old street dog, and Ross, as ever, was picking everything else up. They hadn't employed a new constable, although one was required, mainly because Hope hadn't picked one yet. If she didn't get a move on, Macleod was going to instate one, but it was her team and he wanted her to have the final say on who. There were a few others he could bring in, but it would be a balancing act, as all teams were, and it was Hope's to balance.

He sat down in his chair and pulled over a photocopy of a letter he'd been posted. It had arrived at a care home to Angus McNeil, a former boss of Macleod, when he'd first started out as a PC in Stornoway. McNeil was a hero of his in one sense.

Back then, Macleod thought everything was prim and proper and had its place, and in fairness, McNeil was an excellent police officer. He understood people, and he knew who was lying to him. He could get to the bottom of a problem, but he was also a churchman. A churchman at the time that Macleod looked up to as well. One that kept people in their place. One

11

that set a shining example of biblical continuity, of having systematic doctrine and theology. Now, looking back on it, an incredible habit to stifle anything that truly came from God.

That's the trouble with being older, thought Macleod. *You look back on your life and you realise how often you got it wrong and then you tell the young people they are getting it wrong. But they won't believe you because you didn't believe the oldies back then either. No generation believes the other. Not one of them trusts those who have gone on ahead. In fairness, those who have gone on ahead don't trust the ones coming up behind. That's why each generation made the same mistakes repeatedly. Nothing new under the sun. That's the good book again.*

Macleod laughed a little. He was more chilled out in his faith these days. Not that he held it in any less regard. No, he knew what he believed, and he knew why he believed it. His trust was in his creator, but these days, he didn't try to control other people with it. Certainly not Jane. Then again, he sometimes wondered if God could control Jane. She was a blazing sun, full of energy, and he loved her for it.

His eyes skimmed over the words in the letter again, reading the details of the sexual abuse of a man by another man. It was sickening, and when it came to an end, they killed him. Whoever it was in this tale killed the poor man. Macleod wondered why it had gone to Angus McNeil. Sure, you made enemies when you're in the police, but this was a bizarre letter to send. You might send a death threat, but this was about a minister. Clearly, the letter said it was a minister.

Angus wasn't a minister; he was an elder. You'd have to be thick to get that wrong. Where Macleod had grown up, there was a distinction, a dog collar for a start. He read the letter again, front to back three times over, and then put it in an envelope and placed it on one side of his desk. He didn't want anybody to read it by accident, for it wasn't pleasant. But what was the point of it?

Downstairs, Hope was at the coffee machine, having stepped out of her small office into the larger office of the team. She was still getting used to occupying that office. It had always been Macleod's. Seoras had worked from there, and now she would traipse up the stairs to talk to him.

He didn't seem to want to come down, saying this was her room. If the DCI came down when Seoras was a DI, he always felt agitated, always wondered what he was doing. She remembered some of those DCIs. Seoras wasn't an idiot. Seoras was more than helpful, and he only ever came with good reason. She'd happily welcome him on any day of the week.

'Did you see it?' asked Ross.

'See what?' said Hope, lifting the coffee to her lips, taking a sip. 'The kidnap, it was live on the telly. They just grabbed this guy, four of them. Really bold. Knife in the shoulder. Threatened the rest of the crew and off they went.'

'Where?'

'Not far outside Inverness. It's just crazy. You wouldn't believe it, on live TV. Of course, the cameraman, he just keeps going. He filmed it all. I mean, it's great footage.'

'Oh, well, somebody will be working hard today then,' said Hope.

'Did you see it?'

Hope turned to see that Ross had fired the question at Clarissa, who was plodding into the office. Her tartan shawl was around her, but Hope thought it looked slightly dishevelled. She saw Clarissa had jeans on as well as the shawl

13

was removed and hung up. There was a T-shirt underneath.

'Are you all right?' asked Hope.

Ross burst out laughing and Hope saw Clarissa give him dagger eyes. 'She'll be wanting some coffee,' said Ross.

'Do you want coffee?' asked Hope.

There was nobody else in the room, just the three of them, and Hope felt it would feel so empty if any of them left. There was space for about six people to work there. Only two of the desks were occupied. That was normal. They used to have three out here, plus whoever else was being thrown in on an investigation. Now, they were investigation-less and were tidying up loose ends on older cases. Helping with evidence to go to those who would prosecute previous cases or filing away investigations that weren't cases at all.

'Coffee,' said Clarissa. 'Coffee now!' She sat down in the seat and Hope saw that the T-shirt was hanging loose. Clarissa had no makeup on, or rather, she had makeup on. It was just that makeup had been on for a long time.

Ross jumped up, walked over, grabbed the mug, and poured a coffee. Hope watched as he placed it in front of Clarissa, and she gave another scowl. 'Why does this say "Wake up Grumpy" on the side? I'm telling you, Als, I'm going to go for you today.'

Ross laughed, turned, and almost skipped back to his chair.

'Am I missing something?' asked Hope.

'Nothing. Just not feeling the best,' said Clarissa.

'She was out last night. She was out on a date.'

He was like a little kid, but Clarissa raised her eyes.

'Who?' asked Hope.

'That greenkeeper, Frank, the guy from the golf club who drove the buggy. You know she's back golfing, don't you?'

'What?' said Hope. 'You're back golfing?'

'I like golf,' said Clarissa, and then reached into her bag, pulling out several paracetamol tablets. She ignored further jibes from Ross, then she swallowed them with a slurp of coffee. Clarissa sat at her desk, staring forward as if somebody had flicked the off switch at the rear of her.

'And?' said Hope.

'And what?' said Clarissa.

'Did you bag him?' asked Ross.

'Enough from you. I'm the senior officer here and I'm telling you to shush.'

'And I'm the senior officer in the room,' said Hope, 'and I'm telling you to tell us what happened.'

'I wouldn't have got this from Macleod. Macleod had an air of discretion. He could see when private life shouldn't be brought out in front of colleagues. You could learn that from him, Hope.'

'He would just ask me afterwards,' Hope retorted.

Clarissa raised an eyebrow. It wasn't true, Macleod didn't ask unless he thought it affected the team.

'We had dinner,' said Clarissa suddenly. 'We had dinner, we saw a show, and then, well, let's just say we've had an enjoyable time.'

'But you're in jeans,' said Ross. 'I don't think we've ever seen you in jeans. In fact, I thought you had the jeans and the T-shirt stored in your car in case we ended up somewhere doing a search through muck. You said to me that those jeans and T-shirt were there so that your other stuff didn't get mucked up. You said…'

'I said you were to shut up,' said Clarissa. She slurped her coffee. 'Okay. We went out, we went back to his, we had a great time. I didn't make it back into my flat in time. All right,

15

yes, I've got the search clothes on. All right?'

'Way to go,' said Hope. 'Proud of you here.'

'Shut up,' spat Clarissa. She downed her coffee, stood up, and marched over for another one. Hope's phone rang in her office.

'Excuse me,' she said, and tore off into her own office, picking up the phone from the wrong side of the desk. 'This is McGrath.'

'It's the desk sergeant. Inspector, we've come across a body on waste ground, just south of Inverness. Not very pleasant. We believe it's male, probably of a slightly older age and it's covered in dog faeces.'

'It's what?'

'Covered in dog faeces.'

'You mean like…, dogs have pooed on it?'

'I'm just telling you what the report said, it's covered in dog faeces. I do not know if they were there at the time. It's not normal for dogs to do that.'

'No, it's not. Give me the address.' Hope took it down on a piece of paper, folded it up, thanked the sergeant, and went back into the main office.

'Right, we've got a dead body. Wasteland, south of Inverness. Get the car ready, Ross. Clarissa, pull yourself together. It's time to get to work. I'm going to tell the big boss where we're off to.'

Big Boss. They didn't tell him he was called Big Boss. It was just a comic name for him now that he was upstairs. But Hope missed him. She missed Macleod sitting in that other room. He was a friend, but he was also a professional help. She always had such security in what he said and how he carried investigations, even when they'd argued about things. You could always rely on Macleod to come through.

Hope traipsed up the stairs and saw Lorraine at her desk, outside his office.

'Is he available?'

'Nobody in, go right ahead.'

The first few times Hope had come up, Lorraine had knocked on the door and introduced her. Now the woman realised that Hope was never someone that Macleod needed warning about. Neither were the rest of the team. However, she had seen Lorraine stall people before.

She was good for him. He'd lost Ross. As much as Macleod wouldn't like to admit it, Ross had been the mother hen, the one sorting out all the children so that they could do their activities. He'd got a new mother hen now, albeit she looked very different. Hope knocked on the door and opened it, striding into the office.

'Hope,' said Macleod, 'what do I owe the pleasure?'

'Got a job. Uniform have found a body in wasteland south of Inverness. It's covered in dog faeces.'

'Dog faeces?'

'Yes. Ross is just getting the car now. I'm taking the team out just in case you're looking for us.'

Macleod stood up, turned, and looked out of the window. It wasn't the view he used to have, but old habits die hard.

'Dog faeces. You're sure it's dog faeces?'

'I haven't been out there, and Jona hasn't tested it, but Uniform said it was dog faeces over the body.'

'Would you mind if I came with you?'

'Why?' asked Hope suddenly. It was just a body. He'd been quite happy to let Hope run investigations with just one body. It wasn't national news, not a big deal yet. Not at a point where

17

you'd expect a DCI to come in and take over, since the team had grown massively.

'Just something that I received the other day. I want to check it out and see if it's relevant.'

'Do you want to tell me what it is?'

'No. Well, it's a letter but I will not tell you the contents yet. I'm not telling anyone. We'll have a look. You do what you do, and when you've done what you do, we'll talk about my letter and see if it's important.'

'I'll tell Ross to take Clarissa then. I'm not sure she's going to drive that well.'

'Why, what's up?'

'She bagged herself a groundskeeper last night,' said Hope, smiling.

'Not...,'

'Frank. Yes, she bagged Frank from the golf club.'

Hope could see Macleod smile. At first, it was that warm, happy-for-someone smile. Then there came a slightly devilish grin.

'You go with Ross,' he said. 'Clarissa can drive me. Got a few questions for her on the way.'

Chapter 03

Hope and Ross pulled up in Ross's car, amazed to see that Clarissa and Macleod were already there. They'd left after them with Clarissa looking very much the worse for wear, but now the pair of them were observing the scene. Police tape had marked the scene and the forensics unit was arriving. Hope could see Jona beginning to organise. She marched over to the police sergeant currently organising the scene.

'Hope,' he said.

'James,' said Hope, recognising the sergeant from the station. 'What have you got for me?'

'Older male, possibly sixties or seventies, dressed in minister's clobber. Appears to be covered in dog poo. The smell's rank. There's shit everywhere. Miss Nakamura has just turned up, so I was going to liaise with her and see what she wants done with the scene first. I notice the DCI is here. He hasn't approached me yet.'

'It's okay. He's coming with me,' said Hope. 'Any idea at the moment what killed him?'

'I haven't touched him. The officers that found him checked for signs of life. Paramedic came out and pronounced life extinct. He walked away and left it as it is.'

'Who found him, though?'

'Routine patrol. They were driving past, saw a lot of birds swooping around. Almost a million flies when they got closer because the weather has been so warm. When they approached, they said that the flies all just took off. It was like something from the plague. But they recognised there was a body and called it in.'

Hope looked around her. 'Do the patrol come past here often?'

'They were coming out of the station. This is one route they would take, especially if they were heading out to other parts of Inverness. So, absolutely. Probably pass by here three, four times a day.'

Hope pondered on this. 'Was the body meant to be discovered then?'

'I'll tell you something though,' said James. 'Minister's outfit. The guy on the telly who was grabbed was in a minister's outfit. It could be him.'

Hope thanked the sergeant and approached Jona Nakamura, who was coming out of the rear of her van. She was kitted from top to toe in her forensic smock. 'Can I join you for an initial look?'

'Of course. What's the big boss doing with you?'

Hope grinned. Every time somebody said 'big boss' it made her laugh, because if Macleod knew, he would pull such a face.

'He's got something that may be related to this.'

'You better get him to come over to look at it, then. If you don't, and you think it is something, you'll go back, he'll ask you questions, then he'll come and pester me for a look when I'm in the middle of trying to work. Go get him.'

Hope turned, walked over to Macleod, and told him that

Jona said he should just come and look now.

'Is this because she was afraid that I'm going to pester her later when she's trying to work?'

'Yes,' said Hope.

'She never says that to me,' he said. 'Never. It's always not a problem when I ask but her face, it always says different.'

'It must be that fear you instil in people,' said Hope. She turned before he could even reply. 'Clarissa, you want to have a look too?'

'Dear God, no. But guess I have to.'

'Sergeant,' said Hope, 'with me.'

A few minutes later, Hope, Macleod, and Clarissa were all kitted up and ready to join Jona Nakamura at the scene. They approached slowly, and a waft of dog faeces assaulted their noses.

'Oh, dear God, no,' said Clarissa. 'What the hell? That's…'

'It's dog faeces,' said Macleod.

'I don't know if that's worse than the smell of a dead body.'

'The body has not been dead that long,' said Jona. 'If it had been, given the recent heat we've had, well, you'd possibly smell it over the faeces. I would suggest that these faeces are older than the body.'

Macleod looked over at her. 'You can tell that without even seeing the body, without getting that close?'

'You've got to use your nose sometimes, Inspector.'

They approached, Clarissa squeezing her nose firmly shut. Jona looked down at the body beneath. They stood back while photographs were taken. Then Jona reached down and moved aside some of the dog poo. The body underneath was wearing a minister's black jacket, trousers, and dog collar. Jona quickly pointed out that there were several gaping holes in the

21

trousers.

She slowly peeled back where the fabric had been ripped around the bottom of the minister. The other three turned away. Jona did what all the good forensic examiners needed to do by continuing to probe and examine. She stood up after a moment and walked a little distance away.

'I haven't turned him over yet, but he was possibly raped. Certainly, sexually abused.'

'Anally raped,' asked Macleod.

'Yes, Inspector. Although I'm not sure about some elements of it. I'll need to get him back into the laboratory to get you a more detailed analysis.'

'Do we have a photograph,' asked Hope, 'of the man who was kidnapped?'

From behind her, she heard a shout from Ross.

'I have one here,' he said, still standing back beyond the cordon.

Hope walked to him and brought his phone over. She held it up in front of the other three.

'What do we think?'

Jona took it, approached the body again and eased the head, turning it towards her. She came back a moment later.

'I think that's him,' she said. 'We need to do a more thorough ID check but, yes, that's him. Though, I'm a bit worried. There's something wrong with the jaw. It's been forced somehow. It's not where it should be. To be quite honest, somebody seems to have done a job on this guy. This will not be pleasant.'

The sun was coming up now, and the scene was only going to get warmer.

'That dog poo, though,' said Jona, 'I mean, that dog poo has been dumped on him. This isn't a lot of dogs coming over and doing their business. You'd realise that if you look at it.' She marched forward, picked up a small lump and brought it back, and held it in front of the other three. 'Look,' she said, held it to her nose and took a sniff before holding it before them. 'Sniff that.'

'Dear God,' said Clarissa. She turned away and Macleod heard her vomiting.

'Clarissa had a rough night. She will not be smelling that,' said Hope.

Jona held it up to Macleod. He bent forward, sniffed it and pulled a face like he'd just eaten a sour lemon.

'It's not as pungent. Also dried and firmed out. It's not squishy, so not dog poo that's been laid recently. I would have said, without doing any tests, that this is at least a day old, possibly two.'

'So, he collects dog poo,' said Hope. 'I mean, some guy walking around with those little green bags just waiting for dogs to poo somewhere so he can dump it on top of this guy?'

'Kennels,' said Macleod. 'Kennels have got to collect up poo. You just don't let the dogs poo anywhere. What do they do with it? It's got to go somewhere, hasn't it?'

'And you'd get a load of shit together all at once,' said Jona.

'Yes,' said Macleod, almost testily. 'There'd be plenty of dog faeces about. I'll go talk to Ross, see if he can find out anything.'

Macleod turned away. Jona looked at Hope. 'Did I say something wrong?'

'He doesn't like that sort of language. I thought you knew him by now.'

'What language? It's shit. It is shit.'

'No, it's faeces to Seoras.'

23

'He can tell that to the people that have to sweep it up. They'll call it shit. Anyway, I've got to get on. I'll see if I can pull the medical records of the guy that was kidnapped. What was his name?'

'Hugh Barkley. Reverend Hugh Barkley.'

'Well, I'll pull the records and see if I can identify him, make sure that's him, but from the photograph, it looks like it. It looks like he's been seriously abused.'

'Okay. I'm going to keep the public well back, and the press. The kidnap story is already there, but if they find out he's dead, they're going to jump up and down. So, tell everyone to keep it under wraps.'

'Oh, by the way,' said Jona, 'it's not like Clarissa to have a hard night.'

'I didn't say she had a hard night. She had a good night,' said Hope.

'With who?' asked Jona.

'Frank Macleod.'

'The greenkeeper?'

Clarissa arrived back, looking very white. Jona slapped her on the side of the arm. 'Frank Macleod, you sexy devil,' said Jona, laughing.

'Don't start. Just don't start.'

'Come on,' said Hope. 'Let's start looking into this further. Check the surrounding area as we set up some information-gathering with uniform.' Hope turned away, walking back towards the edge of the cordon. Clarissa turned back to Jona.

'It was good,' she said. 'It was very good.'

Back at the cordon, Hope stripped out of her coveralls before calling over the duty sergeant. 'How many people have you got out here at the moment?'

'Eight,' he said. 'How do you want to play it?'

'Have you got anybody doing stop and question on the road?'

'Not yet.'

'Let's get that done. We'll start searching the surrounding area as well, to see how he was dumped. Somebody's got to come in with a van and a big load of faeces. It might have been seen.'

'When we got here,' said the sergeant, 'the place had been swept.'

'What do you mean?' asked Hope.

'I reckon the van pulled up here on the roadside. They jumped out, deposited him, dumped the faeces on him, got back in the van and somebody swept the gravel here.'

The wasteland was a sea of gravel, small, tiny stones like you would have found in a hard football pitch thirty to forty years ago.

'Do you think it was brushed or something?' asked Hope.

'Swept. Something like that.'

She looked around for her team, caught Ross's eye, and indicated they should gather.

With the four of them there, Hope issued instructions. 'First off, Clarissa, make sure we get uniform sorted and doing stop and ask on the road. I also want any of the local doors to be knocked and questioned because we don't know when this happened. We'll get a bulletin out to the press asking for any witnesses. The sergeant believes that this area has been swept, which is why we're not going to find any footprints.'

'So, you reckon they just came along in a van? You've got to carry that dog poo as well,' said Clarissa. 'I mean, it's got to be smelling, even though it's stored somewhere.'

'It won't be too bad,' said Ross, 'if you wrap it up in the bags.'

'How do you know that?' she said.

'Well, they take those bags, don't they? They wrap up the dog poo in the plastic bags, they tie it tight, and walk past people and people don't go, 'Oh my goodness, they're carrying a load of dog poo. I can smell that for miles.' I mean, the bags must work, mustn't they? And I'm sure you can get a bigger bag than that. They must have them for people who have to clear up loads and loads of shit.'

'Faeces bags,' said Macleod. 'I'm sure they'll be big faeces bags.'

'Whatever we're calling it, let's look at where you can buy them or where you can get them. Let's also have a look at CCTV in the area, see if we can spot vans coming in, Ross. We're assuming that's Barkley. Liaise with those who were investigating his kidnap. Clarissa and Ross, get me more details on him, what he's been doing, why he's ended up dead. We need to get a motive for this. He's been sexually abused as well. You don't sexually abuse a man of that age, I'd have thought, without it being for a very, very good reason.'

'Maybe somebody's got a fetish for a man of that age,' said Ross. 'You can't rule anything out like that.'

'Just get me some detail,' said Hope. 'Well, Jona's working away on what exactly has happened to him. Let's paint the picture behind him. I think you had something as well, didn't you, Seoras?'

Macleod looked up.

'Yes, I got a letter sent to me. The letter had been posted to an Angus McNeil. Angus McNeil was a former policeman on Lewis. He'd since then moved to the south of Harris and to Leverburgh. Unfortunately, he took a stroke not that long ago. He's in a care home down there. He received a letter which, at first, I thought was just somebody having a go at him. Angus was a staunch Free Church elder and the letter he got talked about the rape of a man and the sexual abuse of him. In the letter, the man died. They also covered him in dog faeces.

'I'm going to go to Leverburgh and talk to Angus, to see if there's any connection there. Why send a letter to Angus? Why describe what you're going to do? It's all very upfront and clear. This is how we kill them and then we do it,' said Macleod quietly. 'I need to find out what this really is. In the meantime, follow Hope's instruction and see what you can dig up about Barkley or about how he came to end up here.'

The team broke for a moment and as Macleod sat in the car, he saw Ross field a phone call before calling Hope over to him. Macleod got out of the car and followed him.

'What is it, Alan?' asked Hope.

'Well, we found a burnt-out van three miles from here. I want to say burned down, I mean burned out. It's a crisp.'

'Blast,' said Hope. 'It sounds like they know what they're doing.'

'That's what bothers me,' said Macleod. 'I'm getting the feeling that somebody really knows what they're doing.'

Chapter 04

While Macleod headed for the ferry over to the Western Isles, Ross worked on his CCTV and other media. The electronic trawl to find information belonged to Ross. Clarissa and Hope took Clarissa's green sports car to the parish of Hugh Barkley.

It sat just outside Inverness. Clarissa had called ahead, asking if she could meet the elders of the church. The junior minister of the parish, Jordan Watson, said he would bring them all together. He was meaning to visit them anyway, as they were in shock at their minister being taken. When they arrived at the parish, a young black man stepped out to greet them as they exited the green car. He wore a clerical collar with a black shirt and dark trousers, and gave a respectful smile. He extended his hand to shake first Clarissa's and then Hope's.

'I'm the Reverend Jordan Watson,' he said. 'Do you have any news? We've heard that there may have been someone found near Inverness. They're saying on waste ground. They're saying, well…'

'What are they saying?' asked Hope.

'They're saying he was covered in…, how do you put it?'

'Faeces,' said Clarissa. 'Faeces.'

'Poo,' said the Reverend Watson. 'Terrible. Can you…'

'We can't say anything about that yet,' said Hope. 'Hopefully, we can be more specific about who that is in the future, but at the moment, investigations are ongoing.'

'But these are part of the investigations, I take it?'

The young man wasn't stupid. He turned and indicated that Hope and Clarissa should enter the house.

'I'm Detective Inspector Hope McGrath,' said Hope to him, 'and this is Detective Sergeant Clarissa Urquhart.'

'I have gathered the elders together. Most of my elders don't work,' said the Reverend Watson. 'I forget the church seems to get older, not younger.'

'Well, thank you for bringing them together,' said Hope. 'Hopefully, we won't take too long. We just want to build up an image of the Reverend Barkley.'

'Of course,' he said. 'Inside, please.'

Hope walked through a typical sandstone doorway, so familiar in many Scottish houses, and was then pointed into a living room at the front of the house. Sitting on several chairs were six elders, and Hope felt elder was the correct term. Part of her wondered if there was a defibrillator on hand, but she stopped herself from making any comment.

Clarissa was older than her. Macleod was older, but this lot, they looked like they were ready to meet their maker any day. A round of handshakes began. Hope told Clarissa to take down the names of each of the elders because they were instantly disappearing out of her mind. Once they were seated and coffee had been brought through by the Reverend Watson, he turned and showed that Hope should begin wherever she wanted.

'I'm just hoping, gentlemen, to gain an insight into the Reverend Barkley, what type of person he was.'

'If I may begin,' said a man known as Robert. 'Our Reverend Barkley was a quiet man who's single; he's never had children. He's been a minister for his entire life. When he came here, his CV was quite remarkable. Worked his way up through various parishes, quietly. Very quietly,' he said.

'Is that not what you're meant to do?' asked Clarissa.

'Well, exactly,' said Robert. 'We liked his industry, that he seemed to have time for his parish, for the people in it. He was very good with the kids as well. Very committed in the sense that not having a family, he treated us as his family. He's going to be sorely missed.'

'Did he have any interests?' asked Hope.

'Not that I can think of, no. You would know better, Jordan. You've been sharing the house with him.'

The young man looked to have disappeared inside his shell, but then quickly said, 'He did like to collect decals, an extensive collection of stickers.'

'It's hardly a hobby,' said a man at the end of the elder row. 'Been looking for something interesting about him.'

'Well,' said Reverend Watson, 'I know he did a couple of papers on theological discourse, mainly around the area of same sex marriage, others on sexuality. They weren't big papers. We weren't required to read them,' said Jordan. 'I only did because I was coming here.'

'How was he as a mentor?' asked Clarissa. 'I'm sure he would've been a mentor to you. That's the point, isn't it, in you being here?'

'That he is my mentor, or he was? Is it is or was?' asked Jordan.

'At the moment, we cannot confirm his death, so it's very much is,' said Hope politely.

30

'In that case, he is my mentor. Showed me the ropes of basic life. It's very different here from the Caribbean.'

'I'm sure it is,' said Hope. 'Did you find anything unusual in the way he was as a mentor? Was anything cropping up that was bothering him or concerning him?'

'No,' said the Reverend Watson. 'Not at all.'

'Okay,' said Hope. 'Is there anything untoward in his bank accounts, money? Were there any women in his life? Was there any...'

'We've told you,' said Robert, 'he was totally devoted to here. Spent a lot of time, and more recently, on getting the old church back up, the one they kidnapped him from in front of. That was quite a thing. He did the TV interview rather reluctantly.'

'Any particular reason?' asked Clarissa.

'No, he just didn't like being in the spotlight,' said Robert.

The man beside him coughed, and Clarissa thought she might have to step forward and administer CPR.

As they left the house twenty minutes later, Hope turned to Clarissa. 'Well, quite a bunch.'

'Close to the Lord,' said Clarissa.

'What do you mean?' asked Hope.

'Well, he's bound to be seeing them soon, isn't he?'

Hope didn't laugh, but mainly because the Reverend Watson had hurried up behind them.

'Can I interest you in seeing our church before you go?'

'It's fine,' said Hope. 'I think we've got all we need.'

'No, no, I think you need to come and see the church. It'll be a good idea to see the church.' He turned and shouted back to some elders leaving by the front door, 'I'm just going to show the policewomen the church. It'd be good for them to

31

see where he worked.'

There was a consensus from the elders, but this didn't stop them disappearing off back to their own houses. Hope gave a nod to Clarissa and the two of them followed the Reverend Watson into what was a fairly standard church. There were wooden pews, but there had been cushions put on them and there was the odd tableau hung on the wall. One corner had several pictures from children, and there were crayons and pens, and colouring sheets. It was still a very old church to Hope, but she could see that there had been families in here, even if not that many.

'Forgive me for deceiving you,' said the Reverend Watson. 'I needed to bring you in here. I didn't want to say this in front of the elders because they have a blinkered view of him. They think that the Reverend Barkley is a wonderful man. If I'd said anything negative, they would've jumped all over me.'

'Okay,' said Hope. 'Well, you can say whatever you want to now.'

The Reverend Watson sat down, and Hope watched as he rubbed his hands together, fidgeting, clearly worried about what he was going to divulge.

'Hugh was a solitary individual,' said Jordan. 'I found him rather awkward to be around. He…, well, how do I put this?'

'Whatever way you want,' said Clarissa.

'When I first arrived,' said Jordan, 'I found it very uncomfortable here. He welcomed me, and he was always following me about, shaking hands, and he'd appear in my room with just a towel on, or he'd be knocking at the door when I was in the shower. He was always lingering around me, even when he didn't need to be, more than just someone looking out for you. It was very worrying. The first couple of weeks, he would buy steaks and wine and insist that we sit together, dining together, not outside, not into the village. Just here, but it was…, I don't know if I read it right,' he said.

'I don't know if this is what you normally do, but he was wining and dining me? Is that how you put it? He would get very close. He asked me to play games like Twister, asked me to sit on the sofa beside him. I felt he was making a pass at me.'

'And did you respond?' asked Clarissa.

'No,' said Watson suddenly. 'Where I come from, it's not like here. We don't have the same outlook on society. It would still be heavily frowned upon, two men, and I'm not that way inclined,' he said.

'So, what did you do?' asked Hope.

'I just ignored him. I tried to keep out of his way, and eventually he just stopped. He never stopped looking, but he stopped trying to engineer situations.'

'Well, that's interesting. Did he ever have relations with any other men that you knew of?'

'No, but he was very quiet, kept to himself. He was clever. He had a degree in sociology from Edinburgh before he got his divinity degree. There's a lot of work gone into making that church, the old one, ready for tourists. Lots and lots of funding applications. Hugh's very good at all that, and generally, he's well-liked. There had been no threats to him. I don't understand what's happened,' said Watson. 'I really don't get what's going on.'

'Was there anything else unusual about him you'd like to tell us?' asked Clarissa. She could tell he did because his hands were still rubbing over each other, palm sweating.

'He never watched normal TV.'

'That's not unusual for a vicar, surely?' asked Hope.

33

'No, no, you misunderstand. He watched TV. He just watched nothing that was adult.'

'I didn't think vicars watched adult stuff,' said Clarissa.

'Why?' asked Watson.

'Well, that's naked women and things, isn't it?' said Clarissa. 'He's not meant to support that.'

'No, no, I don't mean pornography. I saying he actually didn't watch adult programs like *Eastenders* or other things from the TV, soaps, or documentaries, nothing. He only watched children's programs, infantile TV. Not at the top end. Further down. The sort of things maybe a seven to ten-year-old would watch.'

'Do you know why?' asked Hope.

'No, I never asked him. I didn't want to engage too much with him.'

'Apart from his making a pass at you,' asked Hope, 'did you ever feel under threat from him?'

'No.'

'Did he have any debt?' queried Clarissa.

'No,' said Watson. 'In every way, he was normal. He was sober. He was very with it, understood how to live a quiet life. We got on okay after those first couple of weeks when he stopped trying to chase me, but it always disturbed me, the way he looked.'

'What do you mean?' asked Clarissa.

'The way he looked at younger people. I have no evidence that he ever did anything, but he just seemed to be always looking. It worried me, and I tried to monitor it, but as he did nothing out of line, I didn't intervene. He said nothing out of line. He didn't act inappropriately. But he watched children's TV.'

'Was he big into children, then?' asked Hope. 'Was he always doing clubs and things?'

'No,' said Watson, 'just the same as any other minister. Nothing in excess, nothing you would say or think he shouldn't be doing that. But I found it very tough trying to work with him.'

'But work with him you did,' said Hope. 'Would you be shocked that someone killed him?'

'No,' said Watson, and Hope stepped closer to him.

'Why?'

'Not somebody from the present time. If somebody from here did it, I would be shocked, but he never spoke about when he was younger. His life seemed to begin when he became a minister. The time before that was never mentioned, not to me. I don't know if he had some trauma or what went on, but I felt there was always something else behind him. It felt like he was always suppressing whatever he was really feeling, whatever he really wanted to do. It felt like it was all held in and never let out.'

On leaving the church, Clarissa stopped at the car and looked at Hope.

'What?'

'Well,' said Clarissa, 'what do you think? I know there's nothing concrete there, but the guy sounds pretty genuine.'

'And he's also somebody without an alibi. He may just be pushing us the other way. That way, he could cover himself.'

'Well, I don't like it,' said Clarissa. 'Barclay sounds too good to be true up here.'

'Indeed,' said Hope, 'but we have found no one who's willing to go after him. We have found no one he's wound up. We're digging into his life,' said Hope, 'and we can't find anyone that

35

doesn't like him.'

'But you heard what he said in there. Reverend Watson believes things happened at the start of his life, moulded him from then. We need to find out more,' said Clarissa, 'go back further.'

'Agreed,' said Hope.

Chapter 05

Macleod had raced for the ferry, barely caught it, and threw some food down him on the way over. He'd taken the run from Uig to Lochmaddy and then driven across North Uist to catch another ferry across the Sound of Harris and arrive in Leverburgh. His plan was he'd drive up to Stornoway that night, stay somewhere and catch the Lewis ferry back the next day.

The care home at Leverburgh was less than half a mile from the Harris-Uist ferry. As Macleod drove off the little roll-on/roll-off vessel, he became deeply nostalgic. Before him, the night sky had not yet arrived despite the late hour. He could see the hills lifting before him. Now living in Inverness, which many considered to be wild once you got outside the city limits, he had forgotten how good the islands looked.

This was home. Something called to him here, and it wasn't cutting the peat, or the smell of it on the fire. It wasn't the community. No, it was something about being amongst all this. The caramel light slicked over the hills, the heather out in full abundance, and the haphazard houses stuck here and there. Was it the lap of the waves as he got off the ferry? He'd been away too long in so many ways and he'd almost forgotten these other parts of the islands, places where he would've come down for a day. Still, he had no time for that; he needed to see Angus McNeil, a meeting he wasn't looking forward to.

Arriving at the care home, Macleod was told by one carer that visiting hours were much earlier and he should come back the next day. Reaching inside his jacket, Macleod pulled out his warrant card, and advised that he was Detective Chief Inspector Macleod. He saw the woman's look of recognition.

'You've been on the telly,' she said. 'I saw you on the telly.'

'Unfortunately, they do film us sometimes,' said Macleod, 'but I need to speak to Angus McNeil. It's an investigation. It's not a social call.'

'If you wait here, I'll see just where he is at the moment, and if we can make a room available. I take it you won't want to be discussing this in public.'

'No,' said Macleod. He sat down in the chair in the entrance hallway and pondered on what had happened. Why talk to a policeman through a letter? Why send something so vile? In none of it was McNeil or any police officer mentioned. It seemed so random, especially to send it to someone who was in a retirement home at the back end of nowhere. For a moment he felt he was being unfair to the place, but relative to the busy world of Scottish cities, Leverburgh was a backwater.

He looked out of the hallway window and could just about see the harbour where he'd come off the ferry. There was a small orange boat there. The lifeboats were such a part of this place, he thought. The lifeboats, the helicopter, all the services were crammed together in such a small fashion. Here in Leverburgh, everybody would know the crew. Everything was so much tighter.

He thought back to when he knew McNeil up in Stornoway.

Everyone on the force knew each other then. You weren't drafted in from the outside so often. You were born there, you lived there, you worked there. It was only his wife's death that drove him down to Glasgow.

'We're ready for you, Inspector,' said the woman.

'Thank you,' said Macleod, rising. 'I'm sorry to bother you at this time.'

'Have you come over from the mainland?'

'Yes,' he said. 'I had to catch the ferry over to Lochmaddy, and then up and across the last boat tonight.'

'Then you'll be needing a cuppa. Can I get you some tea?'

'No. No tea, please. Just coffee if you've got it.'

'Of course,' she said. She turned and shouted something to one of the other carers and then she led Macleod into a small room. There was a table and sitting in an armchair beyond it was a face he hadn't seen in a long time.

Angus McNeil was jowl-cheeked, a bulldog, and when Macleod had first started, he remembered being shouted at by the man. He was firm and had an absolute view of how the Bible would be interpreted and how life should be lived. Angus didn't take any deviation, but in fairness, as a police officer, he didn't enforce his own views on others. But he kept to the law. He could never be bribed, never be tainted, for he was a solid officer, if a little too solid. He didn't really seem to care for the people, much more for the regulations and the rules.

'Angus, it's Seoras.' Macleod put his hand forward, and he saw a fight to recognise him. McNeil didn't lift his hand up.

'You got it then, did you?'

'I did. That's why I'm here.'

'You came all this way for a letter? They must be throwing

39

money at you over there.'

'No, not throwing money,' said Macleod. 'The case I'm working on, all those things in your letter, it's quite possible they've happened to someone.' McNeil looked over and Macleod could see the drool sitting on the bottom lip dripping.

'That's the thing, the world's gone to pot,' said McNeil. 'People just don't get it. You let the standards slip a bit and then the whole rot sets in and you get to things like this.'

Macleod saw the drool drip onto McNeil's shirt. Half his face didn't seem to move well, but that might have been from the stroke. Some people recovered better than others; sometimes they didn't recover at all. Macleod didn't enjoy referring to people who'd been through a stroke as being lucky when they got a little of movement back, but it possibly was. A cup of tea was brought in and placed down in front of Angus.

'This would be white muck, milky mess of a cup.'

'He's awfully rude, Inspector, tells us off all the time. He can't take a hot cup, too likely to spill it, but still gives us grief. Be better giving that grief at the stroke he had. There you go, Inspector, yours is hot.'

Once the woman had left, McNeil slurped on his tea, then he turned and fixed an eye on Macleod. 'The guy that's gone down, who is he?'

'Hugh Barkley,' said Macleod. He got a shake of the head from McNeil.

'Don't know him, never heard of him.'

'When I worked up here,' said Macleod, 'with you, we didn't really have any sexual cases. Were there any others that I wouldn't be aware of from the rest of your time?'

'Not really. Certainly, no sexual attacks. Certainly, nothing that was in that letter. It was all very rough in the letter.'

'It was disgusting,' said Macleod, 'but unfortunately, we see these things.'

'Do you still believe, Macleod?'

'Yes.'

'How do you fathom it, then? How on earth do you fathom it? Look at me. Did I do something wrong? I'm sitting here every day, in and out. Sat here slurping lukewarm tea, sitting looking out one window, day in, day out. Nobody really comes to talk. Sure, I get some visitors from the church and that, but they're not here to talk. They're here to get out again as quick as they can, do their duty. It was always about duty, wasn't it? You see a lot of these modern ones, and they're all about faith and following, but we had a code to stick to, and we had to stick to it.'

'Are you on about the church or the police now?' asked Macleod.

'Police.'

'Do you remember anything, anything about ministers?'

'There was nothing definite,' said McNeil. 'Nothing definite. You always got rumours, but I didn't guess any of them. To be true, never say never in this game. You know that, Seoras.'

'You taught me it,' said Macleod.

'I don't understand why they sent it to me. Did they think I would send it to you?'

'How well do people know us, though? That's the thing,' said Macleod. 'You might talk about me being on the TV, but nobody has my number or my email or mobile, only those I choose to give it to.'

'And those who are too clever by half to nick it,' said McNeil. 'Don't see a computer in here, anyway.'

'Not for me. Too busy slurping my cold tea.'

Macleod watched McNeil twist his head and look out into the corridor beyond. His eyes were fixed on something, and then there came a knock on the door.

'Excuse me,' said a young woman, 'I just wanted to know if you needed anything. He's struggling to sip his tea, is he?'

The woman walked over, took the mug of tea, and started helping it up to McNeil's lips. He slurped a bit, then he choked. Then he told her to put the thing down. She walked over and took some wipes from the corner.

Macleod noted McNeil's eyes. They were never off her, following her until she left. 'It's a sin being in here,' he told Macleod. 'Each day, doing what?'

As she went to leave, McNeil suddenly pepped up. 'Don't forget to take an interest in the good book,' he said. Macleod felt a little awkward. *He's what? Going to evangelise to her right here?*

'You and your book,' said the woman. She turned to Macleod, put out a hand. 'My name's Sarah, one of the helps here, and he's always talking to me about…' And then Sarah stopped, looked at Macleod and went. 'You're that detective.'

'Detective Chief Inspector Macleod. I used to work with Angus.'

'You have that other detective that works with you. I like her,' said Sarah, 'a bit of a role model.'

'Detective Inspector McGrath, Hope. She's done very well for herself,' said Macleod. 'We're all very proud of her.'

'You wouldn't have got a woman doing that in my time. They knew their place then, didn't they, Seoras?' Macleod felt uncomfortable. Back in the day, he would have said so. Not these days, not the way he was, and suddenly he had this dinosaur thrust upon him.

'I wouldn't say that anymore. Women have a rightful place in the world, and they're probably still reaching for it. I can't speak highly enough of Hope.'

'Well, you tell her she's great from me,' said Sarah. 'Anyway, I best leave you in peace. I just thought he looked like he needed something.' Macleod watched as McNeil glared as she walked out of the door.

'I'll see you later,' said Sarah.

'A Jezebel, she's here flaunting herself. She wears those jeans and that top all the time. It's like I've just been put here, Seoras, put here to be tempted until I die. Why? I don't get what I've done wrong. I don't get what I've…'

'Maybe you have done nothing wrong at all. Maybe it's just what is. Anyway, I thought you were a man who enjoyed predestination.'

'That's all right, as long as what's coming is good, if it's not…'

Macleod was hoping for more. Not a trip down a memory lane he didn't want to go to.

'If there's anything else that you can think of in the coming days or even weeks, call me,' said Macleod. He took out a card and put it down in front of McNeil.

'I thought a lot of you,' said McNeil, 'but after that incident with your wife, I never thought you'd get to be a detective, never mind a DCI. You've done well for yourself.'

'Lot of late nights, looking at some of the most awful scenes I've ever known in life, and spending most of the time away from my loved ones. If that's doing well…'

'What loved ones?' asked McNeil.

'I have a partner now.'

'What? Did you marry her?'

'No, she was divorced from before,' said Macleod.

43

'You've fallen. All the fame and fortune gone to your head.'

'No, I haven't, haven't fallen at all. I think I've lightened up. I think I've been enlightened,' said Macleod.

'There'll be a vengeance, a vengeance coming,' said McNeil. 'Fire and brimstone, you mark my words, it will come, and in His day, He'll come and destroy those not with him.' He suddenly thumped his hand on the table in front of him, the tea tipped over. 'There'll be a vengeance. God's wrath will be felt.' He said this last bit so loud that Sarah opened the door.

'What are you doing? Are you all right, Angus?'

'I'm telling him there'll be a vengeance. He's not even married to the woman he's with.'

Sarah turned and looked at Macleod. 'Is she nice?'

'It's got nothing to do with whether she's nice.'

'He always goes off like this,' said Sarah, 'always goes off like this. It's all right, I'll rescue you. You come out with me.'

She turned to walk out, and Macleod caught McNeil looking at her again, eyes fixed on her backside. He turned and put his own fist down on the table.

'Hypocrite,' he said. Maybe he should have left it. Maybe the man, being in a retirement home, should just be left there. After all, he was already hacked off at God for putting him in there, but you had to think of the other people that shared, and had to get on with him.

'You call her a Jezebel, yet your eyes follow her everywhere. You have changed little, haven't you? You were lusty in your ways, then.'

'Get out, Macleod.'

Macleod stood up and followed Sarah out of the room. Once he had left the building, he drove a little way and then stopped at Luskentyre Beach. It was late, but the sun was still keeping the sky honest. Macleod stepped out and took a walk along the sand.

This is home, he thought. *Good sand, hills up around you, moorland, fresh air. This was all home. Why did he feel so out of kilter with it? Would dinosaurs like McNeil ever die? He hoped so. God knew he hoped so.*

Chapter 06

With Macleod away, Hope visited Jona at the morgue for further details on Hugh Barkley. This was her custom. She gave Jona time to carry out a thorough assessment but was called early by her. Jona seemed excited, in that pathologist way, about what she'd found.

Hope walked the corridor down to the rather bland looking offices of Jona Nakamura. She rapped politely on the door of the main office and opened it to see in the far corner that Jona's own office was occupied. Several heads flicked up, and appreciative nods came Hope's way.

It was all very different from when she'd moved up. She'd started off, of course, in Glasgow, there meeting Macleod, and they had flown out to the Western Isles for their first murder investigation. Since then, Macleod had pushed for her and got a unit working out to Inverness.

The city girl was gone, mostly. Inverness was a more open city, not as busy as Glasgow. Hope enjoyed the surrounding countryside, but more importantly, she'd found her man. Not the fireman, not the doctor, not the everyday hero that she thought about when she was younger, but a car hire firm manager. She grinned to herself as she knocked on Jona's door. She'd also found a wonderful friend in Jona Nakamura.

With a shout of 'come in', Hope opened the door and saw Jona's head buried in a mass of paperwork. She looked up and smiled at Hope. 'You will not believe this one.'

'Really?' said Hope. 'I know it was strange. They covered him in all that dog poo.'

'Faeces, yes. We confirmed it is dog faeces and also confirmed that it's come from local kennels. Apparently, they had their excrement stolen.'

'That seems a bit much, doesn't it?' said Hope. 'It also seems that there's many more than one person to play. There's the four doing the kidnap. You just don't run in and grab faeces as a single person. It's becoming quite worrying.'

Jona jumped up from behind her desk, grinning, but as much as she marched out of the office, head and shoulders held high, she was still a good foot below Hope. As Hope followed her out to the morgue, she felt everyone almost laughed at them.

They looked so different. With Jona's Asian complexion and small height compared to Hope's tall, white skin, and red hair, two very different people you couldn't imagine. Yet, they seemed to have common interests. Before John, her partner, had come on the scene, Hope and Jona had been very close. Though Jona had moved back to give Hope and John the room needed for any normal relationship, the two women remained close.

Jona opened the door to the morgue, shouted over to one of her colleagues, and a body was taken out of storage and placed down on the table. It was uncovered, and Hope stood trying to look impressive, not flinching against the gruesome sight before her. The smell was still strong of dog poo. However, Jona seemed unaffected and put on a pair of gloves and a mask before pointing out parts of the body of Hugh Barkley.

'The thing is, Hope, he was interfered with.'

'You said that at the scene, you thought he was sexually interfered with.'

'It's quite clear now, especially around this anus. I've not been able to pick up any semen or anything like that or any other bodily fluids.'

'No sign,' said Jona. 'Bodily fluids were not used. He wasn't sexually abused by a person, at least not by any parts of a person.'

'What do you mean?' asked Hope.

'It's all instrumentation.'

Hope stared at her, slightly bemused, then she realised what she meant. 'Oh, so what they just…'

'Yes,' said Jona. 'A lot of those devices you get in sex shops, they used those, but I would say that they used the large version. The poor guy must have suffered badly.'

'He died like that?'

'No,' said Jona. 'He died from asphyxiation. Something was shoved down his throat that blocked the passageway. I suspect it's the same sort of thing that was used on his backside, but it was shoved in and held down, and eventually, he died. They must have held the nose at the same time. However, it wasn't quick.'

'You're telling me that somebody's taken some sex aids, something like a… what? A dildo?'

'Yes,' said Jona. 'Basically, a dildo. They've abused him with it, then they've killed him by shoving it down his throat and choking him to death.'

Hope's face became contorted. 'That's just wrong. It's sick,' she said. 'Even for what we deal with.'

'It's certainly not normal,' said Jona. 'I'm not the detective, but I think there's a message in what's being done.'

'Do you think?' said Hope. 'Didn't take a detective to work that one out. We'll have to check into the history of Reverend Barkley. See if there's ever been any implications about sexual misconduct.'

'Have you got anything so far?' asked Jona.

'Not much. I know that the young probationer who came in with him to live in his manse felt he was making a pass on him.'

'You think he could have been a homosexual?'

'Possibly, but I don't know. This crime, it looks like it's done by someone who may have been doing this for revenge or out of hate. That's why I'm thinking that if there's something in Barkley's past, even if he's not guilty of it, but suspected. It's the thing about sexual crimes is that they elicit stronger responses.'

'I'm glad you're here talking about this one, Jona. I'm not sure the big boss would be so easy to talk to.'

Hope gave a small laugh. 'No, he wouldn't, but I'm the one who's got to tell him.'

'I can send the report to him. Fire it over the phone, then you wouldn't have to pass on the stronger details.'

'No, I'll tell him. It does worry me, though. We've got four people kidnapping the Reverend. Broad daylight. These people, they aren't afraid. Those are people who seem to know the history, because I doubt you would just grab a random vicar and do this. If you were abused, would you just grab a random clergyman? You'd go for the actual perpetrator, wouldn't you?'

'I'm not a psychologist,' said Jona. 'It's possible they could lash out at anyone. He was a very public figure if he was getting on the TV. Or maybe they're from the local area.'

'It's certainly worth checking,' said Hope. She stared at the figure in front of her, her nose still struggling with the smell of faeces. 'Is there any way,' asked Hope, 'to trace the item? If we find it, are you able to say it's definitely going to be it? Any marks, anything left behind?'

'I'm not sure. Maybe bits that came off it. We can tie DNA that's been left on it. Like you say, they seem to be quite clever. Four of them doing a snatch and grab on live television. You're still struggling to work out who they are.'

'Thank you, Jona.'

Hope disappeared back to the office. She was going to sidetrack and pick up something to eat, but the smell from the body had put her off. It was strange that decomposition or that smell of death was something that she could eat after. But the dog poo was just too much.

Marching into the office, she saw Ross sitting behind his computer with several constables occupying other desks. He was good at organising a team.

'The coffee's on the brew. If you want some.'

'It's fine, Ross. I've got a problem, though. I've just been to see Jona. Hugh Barkley was interfered with, sexually abused with a common dildo. They raped him with it and then put it down his throat, eventually choking him to death on it.'

'Blimey,' said Ross. 'We're looking for people out for brutal vengeance. It wasn't done on a whim, was it?'

'No,' said Hope. 'I need you to look up Hugh Barkley's past. I want to know if there's any type of sexual deviancy, any allegations of sexual misconduct towards anyone. Kids, adults, whatever.' She paused and then asked, 'What's going on at the moment?'

'Been checking up with the Church of Scotland, looking into the career of Hugh Barkley.'

'Don't be afraid to look beyond that. It doesn't mean anything he did was done as a vicar. It could have been done a lot earlier than that.'

'Of course.'

'Especially check up on university days,' said Hope. 'That was when people liked to experiment, wasn't it?'

'Did you go to university and experiment?'

'I went to university,' said Hope, 'but I wouldn't have said my experimentation was quite on those levels.'

She suddenly became aware that the three constables with Ross weren't working as efficiently as they were before, all staring up at her. Of course, Ross wouldn't have been that bothered. The three looking at her now were male.

'Not that it's anybody's business,' said Hope, and glared back at those looking at her. There were coughs and suddenly everyone seemed to be very busy. She flashed her eyes at Ross, who gave her a cheeky grin.

'I'm going to see what the boss has come up with,' said Hope. 'Keep at it, bring me anything you get.'

'Of course,' said Ross.

Hope entered her own office, sat down behind a large desk, and picked up the phone. Macleod would probably be on his way back. He'd arrived late and would have gone that night to the care home. She gathered he wasn't planning to go anywhere until the afternoon ferry.

Hope placed a call. She was struggling to get her mind off what had been done to Hugh Barkley. *What would drive you to do that? What sort of person would you have to be? But more than that, why were there four of them kidnapping him?*

51

'It's Seoras, Hope.'

Hope was impressed. Macleod was never great on phones, but now he could actually recognise when she was calling. The little photograph that Ross had put on was clearly working. He answered to everybody else as Macleod. Well, everybody except Jane, his partner.

'Did you find out anything?'

'No,' said Macleod. 'I'm just heading back up in Stornoway at the moment, dropping in to see if there's anything that jogged my memory. I don't know why it's come to McNeil. He's a washed-up man, bitter, angry. He can't remember anything about any particular ministers or even any case regarding sexual activity like this.'

'Well, it just got stranger,' said Hope. 'Wait till you hear this.'

She detailed out what Jona had told her not long before, but Macleod stayed silent throughout. That was the problem with Seoras. Sometimes you couldn't gauge what his opinion was because he kept it hidden.

'What do you think?' asked Hope.

'What I think is that this changes things. Before we had a dead body, possibly with a statement being made because of the dog faeces thrown on him. Now you've got him sexually abused to death. Plus, you've got the dog faeces as well. We need to look at cases of abuse going back. Anything that we can tie Hugh Barkley towards. They might not have got it right. He may have been innocent. This reaction is strong, very strong.'

'That's what I was thinking,' said Hope. 'They also took him publicly. They could have taken him at the house. If they knew this much about him and what he's done, they're starting off from better than us.'

'Exactly,' said Macleod. 'Also, put an embargo around those details. Don't let it get out. Let them have the dog poo side. That's gross, but it will not send the public on a witch hunt. You bring in the fact he's been sexually abused, and he's a minister. People are going to put two and two together and think about historic abuse cases. Until we have evidence of that, and we know what we're dealing with, we're not bringing that into the public circle.'

'Of course, Seoras. I'll make sure everyone knows.'

'There's one other thing that's bothering me,' said Macleod. 'Why send a letter to an ex-police officer? As far as I know, Hugh Barkley has never been to Stornoway.'

'I don't think he has,' said Hope. 'Ross did dig earlier and his name didn't come up in that direction. Clarissa is off speaking to a Church of Scotland representative. I'll make sure that's confirmed.'

'The question remains, why bother?'

'Sex abuse carried out by the police officer?' suggested Hope.

'No,' said Macleod. 'Really, no. I know Angus McNeil. He was a grumpy sort, but he was an upright person. Proper church elder.'

'Think the eldership could be the linked in.'

'I don't think so, but I am worried there's going to be more. You don't send a letter to someone for one killing. Why do it? Why not just make it all about that other person? Wasn't it just about Hugh Barkley? Why not just kill him there and then on the TV?'

'Because they didn't have time to choke him.'

'Exactly. This is not just premeditated. This is on a level where there's some justice being given back. We need to get on to this one quick because if we don't, I fear there could be a lot more, Hope. One of those things, I can feel it in my blood.'

'Okay, Seoras. Anyway, we'll see you back tomorrow. You grabbing the afternoon boat?'

'Yes, I am. Yes, I'll see you then.'

Hope put the phone down and sat behind the desk, pondering. She turned and looked out the window. *Macleod always did that*, she thought. Then she understood why the familiar scene, that part of Inverness that she'd become accustomed to, was almost a boon. A way of easing you and your thoughts. *Trouble was*, she thought, *Seoras says this is the start of killings, and I really don't disagree with him.*

Chapter 07

The view was stunning. Some architect in the distant past had realised that people who couldn't go far and who couldn't do much should at least get a magnificent view every day. The staff attending to these people would also get a terrific view, making what could be a droll job that bit easier. What the architect didn't know was that former DCI Anthony Henderson could not articulate just what the view meant to him.

Anthony didn't seem to know much these days. He'd been in the police, he remembered that. He remembered colleagues. Why was he here? He thought he'd retired. Certainly, there was a big party that he seemed to be at the centre of. Given that the family never gave him a birthday party, it must have been something to do with work. They'd given him a large card with some comical-looking policeman on it. The card still sat in the room here. Well, not this room, but the room where he slept. He wasn't sure whose house this was, but they were very generous because Anthony got to sit down every day and look out the window. There were boats that went up and down, sailing in and out of the harbour. Beyond that, if you really looked, you could even see the larger vessels, some heading towards the Sound of Mull.

As he sat in his grey corduroy trousers, shirt and tie on, he was fairly happy. He knew that sometime soon he would get fed. While the restaurant didn't give you an option, it at least gave you decent food. There was a pudding with every lunch, and with every tea. The coffee was often cold. He'd asked about that once, and the waitress had said it was for his own safety. He wasn't sure what that meant, but then again, he wasn't convinced about the waitresses.

They wore green outfits, trousers and tops. He thought he'd seen them once in a hospital, but that couldn't be right. Hospital nurses were different, and they had those watches that hung upside down. These people didn't have those. Sometimes he felt like asking them more, but generally, he felt like just sitting back and watching the world go by.

He did well every day, though. He got up, with a little help, and walked to this chair. It was a good chair, and it had a table just beside it where he could have his coffee, even if it was cold. Some man came in twice a week from the church; at least he said he was from the church. Anthony didn't understand why someone was coming into this house from the church, but the man seemed to enjoy it, and so Anthony talked to him.

There was also the man in red who came in. He would come and sometimes put an envelope in front of him. Everybody seemed to get envelopes at one time or another. Anthony wasn't sure how that worked. Did people have his address here, now he'd moved in? At least he thought he'd moved in. He wasn't positive when he'd moved in either. Maybe it was a couple of days.

Anthony spent the next ten minutes watching a boat sailing out of the harbour. He thought it was a fishing boat, but it looked spectacular with the sun glancing off the water beside it. The television was on, but they never showed the good programmes anymore. There was one on previously about some binman. He didn't know if he was a binman. They had these green and blue bins with lids that didn't come off. Bins were metal, sometimes with a silver or a black lid, and binmen carried them on their backs. These binmen pushed things on wheels. It was strange. There were a lot of strange things on that television, that's why he didn't watch it. The boats weren't strange; they just came and went.

'Anthony,' said someone beside him. 'Anthony.'

He turned his head. There was that waitress again.

'We've got something for you.'

'Oh,' he said, 'who's brought that, then?'

'It's Ian. Ian's come with it. The one that brought you the box last time.'

'Oh yes, the box.' It was a present from someone, though he didn't know who. There were socks in it. He didn't need that many socks. People seemed to like to buy him socks.

'When's lunch?' he asked.

'Another hour, Anthony. We'll take you down.'

'What's on the menu today?'

'Beef,' said the woman. 'You like beef, don't you?'

He did like beef. Anthony was very fond of beef. Sometimes they did this foreign food. Spag bol was one of them. He didn't like that. *Just potatoes and meat and vegetables, that was plenty. In the summer, maybe a salad. Yes, life was okay,* he thought.

Ian, dressed in a red outfit, placed something on the table beside him. 'There you go. All right, Squire?' and then he was gone again. Anthony picked up the envelope, and after three failed attempts, ran a nail up across the top of it and ripped it

57

open. He took out the card inside.

It wasn't his birthday. Why was he getting a card? He looked at the front of it. He couldn't make head nor tail of what was going on. The card seemed to jump out towards him, as if what was happening was coming at him, not just sitting on the paper. There were two, what he thought were men, there, one standing in front of the other. They seemed quite happy. Well, at least one did. He opened the card, looked inside. There was nothing. They'd forgotten to write on it. Who'd sent this? He turned around and placed the card down beside him and went back to looking out the window.

Emma Healey hadn't been in the home that long, but Anthony was one of her favourites. He never gave you any bother. He usually said thank you, and you even got the tale of his police days. Emma wasn't sure if he'd blown it all up out of proportion, but the tales were entertaining and the man could generally handle his toilet. Cleaning up poo, or whatever other mess the rest had got into, was not something that Emma enjoyed. She didn't enjoy the job, but it paid okay.

'You've got a card, Anthony. It's not your birthday, is it?'

Anthony gave a shake of his head, but he didn't look at Emma. He just continued to watch boats outside the window.

'Oh well. Can I look at it?' She reached forward and picked it up. 'Oh,' she said, 'what the heck's this? Who sent you this, Anthony?'

Anthony was staring out the window. The front cover had a sexual act between two men. One standing in front of the other was not happy, the other one seemed ridiculously so. The card built out into a 3D image. Emma was not a prude, and she'd seen many of those slapstick cards in the past, what she would have called seaside entertainment, a bit of slap and tickle. They were rude, but this was gross. The image in front of her looked abusive. She opened the card up. There was nothing inside.

Dear God, she thought, *what the hell's the world coming to? Who in their right mind would send this guy this?*

'Anthony, did you look at your card?'

'Yes,' he said, now staring at her.

'What did you think?'

'They forgot to say who they were. I don't know why they sent that.'

Whatever the card was meant to do, it clearly didn't have the desired effect on Anthony. He had placed it down as if it was just another card. As if it said Happy 6th Birthday, an irrelevance to him.

Emma picked up the card and walked down to the supervisor's office.

'Jenny, you seen this? It arrived for Anthony today.'

'Bloody hell,' said Jenny, 'what the heck is that? Is there anything inside it?'

'No.'

'Is he all right?'

'He's fine,' said Emma. 'I don't think he's looked at what it actually is. It's sick though, isn't it? Disgusting. I mean, that guy in the front just looks like he's being... well, he's not happy, is he?'

'No, he's not. Anthony's an old policeman.'

'Are you sure?' said Emma. 'He tells me all the stories.'

'Oh no, he's a former DCI. Sharp in his day. Not anymore, though. Look, if he hasn't been bothered by it, it's probably some prank from people that used to know him in the past. Just bin it. Rip it up and bin it.'

'Okay,' said Emma, 'but if he gets anymore, we probably should ask somebody to come and look at it.'

'Yes. I agree, but it's probably just a prank. Somebody he lifted in the past.'

* * *

As Derek strode on to the allotment, he was particularly impressed by how well the cauliflower was doing. The leaves were enormous, and inside, the precious ball of white had started to form. It wouldn't be that long before it was ready. He tottered along looking at the broccoli, then the radishes, and finally, the beetroot he'd prepared. He loved the allotment, as he could get away from everyone.

His life had been given in service to the Church. A life where he'd had to deal with everyone else's problems, but now he could rest. He'd redeemed himself. He had given God his due, and he was at rest. The Episcopalian Church had not been too bad either, a lot less stuffy. He thought this funny, considering he'd joined the Anglicans when the rest had gone down other routes.

He stood up after checking the last beetroot, turned to walk to his shed, and saw the long, blonde hair of someone he did not want to meet. You'd have thought at his age that people could just let be. Live and let live. That's what it was, wasn't it? That was the whole point, but not Sarah Melbourne. Oh no.

Sarah was a bitter enemy, a confirmed atheist. Derek had no problem with atheists. People could believe what they wanted to. The problem was that Sarah was a zealot. People never thought of atheism as having its preachers, its outreach merchants. Or they said the Church was always out there giving its rallies, giving its conversion message. Atheists had a conversion message too.

Derek had realised this more and more as he grew up within the Church. There were two sides out there pushing you to convert. Those towards there being a god and those to say there definitely wasn't. Most people were hovering somewhere in the middle.

That was the problem with no proof, wasn't it? If you'd just had proof, if God just stood there in front of us and went, 'Hey, this is me. You don't have to worry whether I'm real anymore.' We would all be in the light. Derek tried to walk quietly, but when Sarah turned, he knew he was in for it.

'Is that you back again? I suppose you're hoping that God's blessed those vegetables.'

'I'm just out to enjoy the sun, Sarah. Just resting up.'

The sad thing was that Sarah was still an attractive woman despite the fact she was seventy-two. Some people in life got longevity. Some people were very lucky and got a great complexion. Others kept their mobility. When you reached the later ages, you just didn't know what you were going to get.

Sarah had kept her looks. Yes, there were some crow's feet here and there, the odd blemish, but for her age, she looked remarkable. It pained Derek that seeing her in one sense brought joy in the way a good-looking woman does to a man, but it also caused him to flinch away from her. She was sour and bitter. The sad thing he thought was she could do with God.

'Have you seen what your crowd has done now? They've got that big tent coming next week. I take it you'll be going.'

'I haven't looked,' said Derek, trying not to yawn in Sarah's face. Every time it was this. Every time she went on about it. *Your crowd. You're this, you're that.* He was retired, and he was himself.

He heard the click of the little gate. Sarah's allotment was beside Derek's, but there was a gate between them, and she now opened the latch and pushed it away from her as she entered.

'It's too good a day for this. Can you not just have a drink with me, Sarah?'

'They'll make a mess of that field; you wait and see. You know most of the people that go to those things don't really care. It's not the way evangelism should be done; all hyped up. It's all just show.'

'Well, you seem to evangelise enough.'

'No, I don't.'

'Yes, you do. I've told you before. Look, there's no point to this, Sarah. I've got some lemonade in the shed. Why don't we just sit in silence? Enjoy the place. Despite all your going on at me, I do like your company.'

For a moment he thought she was going to agree, but then she pointed over her shoulder. 'Look.'

'What now?' asked Derek. 'I don't want to argue about things. I don't want to...' A hand clamped on his shoulder. Another hand went round over his mouth and suddenly he was being dragged backwards.

'Derek!' shouted Sarah. She tried to run forward as fast as she could when suddenly she was pushed backward by a powerful man in black. She hit the ground with a sickening crack. Derek was being hauled away, and he saw Sarah lying, struggling. She had been close until the attacker had forced her back. Derek had seen her arm go out. Possibly she'd even grabbed the person, but he wasn't sure.

What he knew was he was going somewhere else. Somewhere he remembered the television and what had happened to Hugh Berkley. His heart sank, and the panic set in.

Chapter 08

Hope McGrath drove around the car park at Raigmore Hospital, circling it several times before finding a space. It got no better. Sometimes she thought she should just walk over from the station, but it would be sod's law that she'd get a call out. Having to respond quickly, she would end up legging it across the road in front of the eyes of the entire station. It was always better to have the car with you, despite the frustration of trying to park.

She had thought she was going to go with Seoras who was returning from the Hebrides. His trip from the ferry was slightly delayed and she couldn't wait any longer. Sarah Melbourne had been taken to Raigmore after the incident in Aviemore, and Hope had contacted the doctors. They told her to give it a few hours before coming in to see the woman. Now, having had the go-ahead to interview her, Hope was optimistic that they might start getting somewhere with this case.

She took the lift to the third floor. Sarah was in a private cubicle. Hope stared at her own image in the mirrored interior, remarkably on her own, where usually the hospital lifts were so busy. It'd been a long time working with Seoras, but these days were seemingly different.

She'd always been a sidekick, the two of them investigating together, but now more and more she went off on her own. Even back in the day when he tasked her with something, it was always the two of them coming together at the head of the investigation. Now, she was often charged with running it, of being that person, with Seoras dropping in to make sure she was steering it correctly.

He hated doing that, she could tell. Same as he had hated when the DCIs came down to pick at his investigation. Sometimes she wondered did he just take the move up to allow her to still be in Inverness. If she'd taken the jump to Detective Inspector prior to his promotion, she might have had to move.

She wasn't sure if he was happy, for he seemed to be involved in more meetings and paperwork these days. For as long as she'd known him, Seoras was happy on the chase, happy out there, although the face never showed it. He had a reputation within the station of being miserable. The number of people who still spoke to him as Sir or Inspector, despite the first name policy the force had taken up, was crazy. They said it without fear, not like Ross. Ross did it out of respect.

While she was on her own, Hope undid her ponytail, gathered her hair again, and pulled it back together. When she was starting on the force, she wore the ponytail all the time, even at home. John always liked her hair undone. He said he always saw a police officer when he saw her with her hair up. Whereas when she came into the house with her hair down, he knew she was off duty, knew she was not obsessed with all that death stuff. She never thought she was completely obsessed, but to be a good detective, you had to obsess somewhat with the cases. Maybe that wasn't a good thing.

The doors of the lift opened, and Hope marched out along the corridor and checked in with the nurse looking after Sarah Melbourne. Having been escorted to a room, she found the woman propped up in bed and looking rather the worse for wear.

'Sorry to disturb you, but I'm DI Hope McGrath.'

'The constables said you'd be coming. They said you'd pop in to talk to me. I'm not feeling the best.'

'Obviously,' said Hope, 'and you've had quite a shock, so I'll keep this as painless as I can.'

'Where's the other one?'

'The other one?' asked Hope.

'The other one. The two of you, you're always a pair, aren't you? I've seen that on the television. You were doing the news conferences, and he'd always be in the background. I always wondered what he'd be like to work with. What is he like?'

They'd become a fixture amongst the Inverness population. Macleod and McGrath, the tall ginger woman taking the press conferences, and this moody older man marching around in the background. But somehow they got the job done.

'Inspector Macleod's now Detective Chief Inspector Macleod.'

'So, he's got all the reward from your success?' said the woman.

'No,' said Hope, 'it's not like that. I'm Detective Inspector McGrath now. I was detective sergeant.'

'Well, good for you. I always thought you were the better one. You know, you could talk to people, the public and that. He's very mardy, that guy. Very…'

'The chief inspector has his ways,' said Hope, 'but he's very good at being a detective. Can we talk about what happened?'

'Oh, yes,' said Sarah. 'They've got Derek. He's the minister.'

'I know who he is,' said Hope. 'Can you take me through what happened?'

'I went down to talk to him, have a word with him about his allotment and his church, and what they do. I'm not at home to them, they're not my sort of thing. Don't believe in all that mumbo jumbo, all that God rubbish. There's nothing out there, is there? Derek spent his life telling people there is, and well, I usually give him a piece of my mind, but I wouldn't have done that to him.'

'No,' said Hope. 'Can you just fill me in on the detail of what happened?'

'Well, they were big. There were four of them. In masks and dressed in black. I mean, I ended up on the ground and broke my pelvis, that's why I'm sitting here, but they were coming for Derek. They were coming for him.'

'What would you say about them?'

'Well, I think there were four of them and one was certainly very large. He was male, that was definitely a man. There's no way that could have been a woman. I think there were two other men and a woman. It was a woman; you saw the curves. You know?'

'Did they say anything?'

'Very little. I wouldn't be able to tell you where they were from. It was all so quick, and I was so sore. I'm still feeling it.'

'Do you know anyone who would have a problem with the Reverend Clark?'

'Well, anyone that thinks he talks nonsense like he does.'

'I meant people who would have a problem with him enough to kidnap him.'

'Well, no, I don't know people like that. But you can upset

people, can't you? You can upset people telling them what to believe, especially when it's all nonsense.'

Hope wasn't particularly religious, but she realised that this woman was on the other side of the coin of the man she was describing. Maybe that's why there was tension.

'But in terms of what he said, the things that people would have a problem with, did you say anything particularly different? Was he particularly hateful towards any group, like the LGBTQ+ group or the Muslim factions or the council or anybody?'

'No, Derek just talked about all that new life and forgiveness and that sort of thing and was very seven-day, that's what he taught. I tried to talk to him about things, but he said little. I didn't like that about him. He couldn't answer the questions.'

Hope wondered if the man had just stayed silent.

'You get a feel for who these people were?'

'The only thing I got to feel was their hair. I grabbed it on the way down. Still had some in my hand, little strands when I got here. I spoke to some doctors.'

'These strands of hair. What happened to them?'

'I said, I talked to the doctors. They came with a bag, and they stuck the hair in the bag.'

'Well, that's interesting,' said Hope. 'I need to talk to the doctor about that. What about the van? Do you remember much about it?'

'I didn't really see much of it. I think it didn't have a license plate on it but I can't be 100% sure. In truth, I don't really want to remember it.'

'Okay,' said Hope, and she made the woman go through her statement again, this time noting down approximate heights of people, but there wasn't that much there. Four people had come in, grabbed Derek Clark, and whizzed him out again.

'You think they'll kill him?'

'I couldn't possibly say. That's why we're investigating, though,' said Hope.

'Well, he deserves it. Talks absolute nonsense. I mean any of those people do, don't they? Anyone that thinks that there's some sort of being out there, platitudes and that nonsense. People telling me who I must worship. No, there's nothing out there, nothing at all. He should have listened to me. He wouldn't be in this mess if he listened to me, wouldn't have that dog collar on and got grabbed.'

Hope was normally good at tuning out rambling interviewees, but this woman was annoying her. She turned to leave and let her foot catch the edge of the bed, causing it to rock. She saw the woman wince.

'Sorry, too clumsy.' As she left the room, Hope saw a familiar figure heading down the hospital corridor. He had his long coat on with a suit underneath, a white shirt, and tie.

'Good trip?'

'No,' he said, 'but that's not important.' Macleod came alongside Hope, looked up and down the corridor, and then seemed to think for a moment.

'Do you want to go downstairs and get some coffee, talk it over?' she said.

'Oh, no. No, no, no, no, no. Go back to your office and talk it over. Any joy from inside there?' asked Macleod.

'No. Got four people, got rough heights. One's a woman, one's an enormous man, but no. She said she grabbed some hair, or she had hair from one attacker. I'm just about to chase up the hospital on that. She said the doctor took it; thought he'd put it in a bag.'

69

'Well, that's helpful,' said Macleod. 'We need to get that, get it to Jona, but I'm thinking, really compare this description, the second grab with the first one.'

Hope could see that Macleod was agitated.

'What is it, Seoras?' she asked. 'It's not just a nasty boat trip.'

'No,' he said, 'we need to look at those, did the first grab and the second, see if they're the same people. What's bothering me is how many people could be behind this.'

'Well, there's at least four, isn't there?'

'There's at least four,' he said, 'but I'm thinking it may be more than that. We don't have any footage of this one. We've only got your witnesses' descriptions, but it's been playing on me. If the four people were different, how many people are behind this? Is this a group, a society? Is this something more than just a…'

'Just a what?' asked Hope. 'They're taking ministers and killing them, or at least they've killed one. It looks like an attack on the clergy for abuses carried out. I've tasked Ross with looking into the history of Derek Clark. We need to try to trace if he's got any connection to Hugh Berkley.'

'They're different churches, Hope, different churches. They don't mix that well. Episcopalian and Church of Scotland. Well, you might come together for service and that, but they're not working alongside each other. It seems strange, and why would you attack different churches if you had a problem with abuse? It's just too general. The idea they're just attacking vicars or priests or ministers just because it's the church, it's too general, too big.'

'Okay, Seoras,' said Hope, seeing he was agitated. 'Are you okay?'

'No,' he said. 'We've also got this missing minister. We need something to tap into. Let's get this hair sample.'

'You go downstairs, I'll join you in a minute,' said Hope. 'Get the coffee as well.'

'I'm not buying coffee from here.'

'What's wrong with the coffee?'

'You know,' said Macleod.

'Well, you have a bottle of water then. I want a coffee. See you in a couple of minutes.'

Hope marched off and got the nurse to point her towards the doctor looking after Sarah Melbourne. He advised he could pick up the bag which he'd stored away with the hair. A couple of minutes later, Hope entered the café at the front of Raigmore Hospital, sporting a little plastic bag.

'Going to get that over to Jona,' said Hope, sitting down opposite Macleod. She saw a plastic cup in front of her with some coffee in it. Macleod was indeed holding a bottle of water. She took a drink and watched Macleod as he picked up the bag with the hair sample and sat staring at it for the next two minutes.

'If we don't get a DNA match in the records,' he said suddenly, 'this won't make a difference, will it?'

'Well, let's hope we get a match. We'll be able to start somewhere because at the moment we're struggling.'

'You won't get one,' said Macleod. 'We won't get one. If they've had their hair grabbed like this and we know they're killers, you'd just despatch the person. You wouldn't leave them with hair in their hand. It makes little sense unless...,'

'Unless these people haven't done it before, unless these people are amateur or are just very clever,' said Hope.

'You'd better get that back,' said Macleod. 'Where's Clarissa?'

'Off to the home of Derek Clark, went to see his wife. She

checks that out. Ross is checking the church and his career, and I came over here to see our witness. She's not in great shape but...'

'Maybe I should interview her as well; maybe I'll get a different take.'

'No,' said Hope, thinking that would just create some sort of powder keg in the room. She wasn't sure Macleod would take the woman's atheism with good nature.

'There's something being said,' Macleod suddenly blurted. 'Why are they sending this letter to say... Look, they haven't put their name on it. There's nothing to say, "This is us. This is why we're doing it, so why bother sending the letter in the first place?"'

'We'll get them,' said Hope. 'Don't worry, we'll get them.'

Chapter 09

The little green sports car turned left off the A9 towards Aviemore. Despite the darkness of what had been going on, Clarissa was in a good mood. She had told Frank that she was now working, and unfortunately, after their time together, she could be working very late and struggling to see him. Clarissa had said to him in a brief note that this was normal, and if he really wanted to know what it was like, he could talk to one of her colleagues' partners. She'd popped home only briefly for a change of clothes and was surprised to find flowers on the doorstep. A little white card said, 'When you're ready, when you have the time, I'm ready too.'

Clarissa had been lonely. She'd recognised it in herself. She wasn't one of these women who in older life didn't feel the need for company; either some sort of platonic relationship or a life of independence. That wasn't her. She almost said there was life in the old dog, but she wasn't an old dog. Sure, in work she was a Rottweiler, but work was different.

Frank had been charming the other evening, and they danced. She hadn't danced in years, but she remembered how to do it. She moved with the beat. He'd also pushed nothing, no agenda, just chatted and talked, and danced, and made it

73

fun. That was the trouble with this job, often there wasn't any fun. She let go a smile, which probably disturbed some drivers going the other direction, but Clarissa was feeling happy.

She was feeling buoyed. *I am* - she stopped for a moment - *back in the game*. Sounded cheesy, didn't it? It sounded like you were some sort of hot gigolo. Yes, she thought, I'm back in the game. She laughed out loud as she drove along, again another sight that must have been disturbing. She didn't care.

Soon she passed the small Episcopalian church where Derek Clark would have taken worship. The house was two streets away, and as she pulled up in front of it, she saw that all the curtains were closed. Parking her car at the front of the house, she strolled out in her boots, trews, and shawl. Clarissa forced a more demure aspect instead of grinning like the Cheshire cat that had driven the green car to this point.

She knocked on the door, and it was opened by a woman of average build. However, she wore a long skirt which was hung on hips that barely emerged on the side of the woman. The skirt was black, and there was a grey top, mundane in aspect, with only a small chain hanging around the neck, a tiny cross coming off it. Her hair was tied up in a bun at the back, a mix of blonde heading to white. Clarissa saw dark spectacles sitting on the end of a nose that was built for them.

'I'm sorry to bother you at this awkward time, ma'am, but I'm Detective Sergeant Clarissa Urquhart.'

'Yes, somebody said you'd be visiting. Do come in. I've kept the curtains closed because really we don't want any fuss.'

'No, indeed,' said Clarissa, walking into the house and then down a rather neatly decorated hallway.

'Go through right to the back,' said the woman. 'Would you like tea?'

'Don't put yourself to any trouble,' said Clarissa. 'I'm just here to ask a few questions. It's obviously a very disturbing time for you.'

'Of course it is,' said the woman, 'but we can have tea. Please, go on.'

Clarissa was urged through a door at the end of the hallway, which led to a kitchen, but was then pushed further past another door. Once through there, she found herself in a room lined with books.

'This is my sanctuary,' said the woman. 'I sit in here and read. Over the last day, it's been very good to me, kept me away from any nonsense. The constable that came round said it was an ideal thing to do. You can't see it from the front of the house or anywhere else. It's quiet and relaxing. I'll make you your tea.'

The woman stepped out, and Clarissa walked around the room, staring at the various books. Most of them were academic, formal, certainly not what Clarissa would've read. She liked a bit of spicy romance, not that she devoured books. In her own collection were serious tomes, mainly about the art world, but she didn't live in a book for her art interest. She wanted to see the art. She may have been prejudging the woman, but this looked like somebody who embraced the world through a book as opposed to through the objects themselves.

The door into the room suddenly opened, and the woman walked in carrying a large tray with China teacups and teapot.

'Please, sit down.'

Clarissa did so in an ornate chair that she found not overly comfortable. It had a very straight back, and Clarissa was someone who liked to lounge, especially when she was relaxing.

'Milk, sugar?' asked the woman.

'Just black,' said Clarissa. She didn't want to offend the woman by saying she'd rather have a cup of coffee, and instead took a China cup with what she thought was the weakest tea she had ever seen. 'Anna Clark, isn't it?' said Clarissa.

'Yes, yes, I'm Anna.'

'You seem to be doing rather well, considering the worry that must be on your mind.'

'Well, to be honest, he's away a lot, and he'll come back. Derek's usually not about, so it's not something that I'm really missing at the moment, maybe in a week if he doesn't.'

'Are you aware of the Reverend Hugh Barkley?'

'That's that poor unfortunate vicar that died, isn't it? Terrible.'

'You know Derek was taken in the same vein, apparently?'

'Well, we'll have to wait and see for that. Like I say, it's strange.'

'Was he down the allotment a lot?' asked Clarissa.

'Regularly, yes. I suppose you people will find out who did it in the end. Hopefully, we'll get him back.'

'Yes,' said Clarissa. 'Hopefully so. You say that Derek was away a lot?'

'Yes, with the church. He's usually back for services on Sundays. He has certain things he has to do.'

'Are you heavily involved with the Church?'

'No. No, I think quite modern, really, aren't we? I think these days it's no longer expected to see a vicar's wife heavily involved.'

'Okay,' said Clarissa. 'And are you aware he was down at the allotment when it happened?'

'He spends time down there. I'm not a gardener. I like my books.'

Clarissa stood up, walked around the room, and realised there were no pictures. When she'd come through the kitchen, there'd been none either.

'Do you mind if I pop out to my car? I think I've forgotten something,' said Clarissa. 'You don't have to get up. I'll find my way there and my way back. It's not a problem.'

'Okay,' said Anna, and she turned and grabbed a book off the table.

Clarissa thought it was Latin and ignored the woman walking out through the kitchen. But instead of entering the hallway, she took another door into other rooms. Quietly, she walked through the entire house. She couldn't find a photograph of the pair of them. There were barely any photographs of Anna, and next to none of Derek. The few that there were, they were with other people.

Marching back out to her little car, Clarissa picked up her phone and called Ross.

'Als, how's it going with the investigation? Anything to do with the church? Anything?'

'Well, I've got his finances up in front of me. I can't find anything particularly weird.'

'Apparently, he's away a lot. That would throw up a lot of expenses, I would think, especially if he was away on church business. Are there any payments coming through that you can see that are beyond the normal salary?'

'No, the stipend looks fairly straightforward; once a month.'

'There's nothing in terms of what he's buying that shows him to be away from Aviemore a lot, maybe other parts of the country?'

'No. From what I've got here, he seems to be rarely away, very rarely, and those I've talked to within the church seem to think that he's a quiet, bog-standard vicar. The sort that does the services, doesn't rock any boats, doesn't make any political statements. Not looking for a promotion. Solid chap, as they would put it. One you can put to a place, know he'll do his duty, but that's about it. He'll cover off the service and visit the sick, if they have them. That's the image that's coming back to me.'

'Okay, Als. Have you got the phone list? Are there any calls he's making out from the house phone or even a work phone?'

'I've got them in front of me. Do you want it?'

'No. Thing is, I've been talking to his wife and, well, you wouldn't know it's his wife.'

'Well, not everybody's going to be as lovey-dovey as you and the new man.'

'Shut up,' said Clarissa. 'I'm being serious. Look, I'm struggling to find a photograph of the two of them together, yet they're clearly living in the same house.'

'Did you find a double bed?'

'Yes, I did, but I also found several single beds. There was no evidence that they stayed in the same room.'

'You didn't check for clothing?'

'I'm popping out to the car here and she's not a suspect, so—'

'Well, from phone calls and that, there's nothing I can see.'

'Okay. Tell you what, don't go anywhere. I'm going to call you back soon. I might need your help.'

Clarissa closed the phone call and walked back into the house through the open front door. She found Anna Clark sitting, reading the same book that she'd picked up when Clarissa left.

'Anna, do you mind putting that book down? I think we

need to have some serious discussion here.'

'What do you mean?' asked the woman. The book slid slightly off her lap, but it certainly wasn't put away.

'Thing is, and I apologise for this, but I've just walked around your entire house. I can't find a single photograph of you two together. I'm half inclined to go up to your bedroom and see if there're clothes from both of you in it.' The woman looked a bit shocked.

'The problem is,' said Clarissa, 'if I do, it makes you a suspect. You're not close to him. He could be a problem in your life. For some reason, there's a falling apart. I need to know what's going on between you, so I don't have to drag you down to the station and try to work it out.'

'It's very astute of you,' said Anna. 'I guess that's why you're detectives. I have a sham marriage,' she whispered. 'It's not one we entered lightly. Derek needed it for an image, as he put it, to be a vicar. I just needed help with the bills and to keep other people off my back. In society it's good to be married, isn't it? Or at least it was. It's worked for us. We share the bills in the house. We keep ourselves to ourselves. The only time we talk is if we need to know where the other one is in case someone asks. I'll not be evasive. The thing is that Derek and I are practically strangers. I don't know an awful lot about him, and he doesn't know an awful lot about me. I could probably tell you what he eats because we share the kitchen, but we cook our own meals. We manage our own money, and we have an arrangement where the bills that are in common, we break down and pay.'

'Okay,' said Clarissa. 'If that's the case, would you know of anybody who would want to harm him?'

'I would struggle to know of anyone who actually wants to

talk to him, anyone who is his friend, or anything about him. I'm afraid I can't be of use to you.'

'Do you share a phone?' said Clarissa.

'Well, not the mobile ones, but we have one for the house.'

'Has anybody ever called on it you found to be strange or suspicious?'

'No, I rarely use it. I rarely pick it up if Derek's not in. To be honest, I'm not sure why we have it except that Derek needs it for church.'

Clarissa pulled out her phone, excused herself, and called Ross.

'Have you got those phone numbers?'

'Yes, I have.'

'Have you got any that are repetitive? Because I've got Anna Clark here and I think you should run through the repetitive ones with her. I've got a suspicion about something.'

'Okay,' said Ross. 'Put her on.'

Clarissa watched the woman answering questions from Ross. He went through several numbers with her, asking her each time and getting a murmured, 'no.' Occasionally she advised that the number was the doctors, or was such-and-such a person from the church, but there was one number that kept coming up. When Anna Clark handed the phone back to Clarissa, she could hear the excitement in Ross's voice.

'One number,' said Ross. 'There's one that keeps coming up. It's phoned, outgoing, never incoming, and Anna knows nothing about it, but I do. Apparently, the phone is registered to a Samuel Benoit, and he lives in Feshiebridge. Seems a little suspicious.'

'Indeed, it does,' said Clarissa. 'Come out here, Als, with me. Check with the boss, but I want you down with me before we go anywhere on this. If this is a phone number off to something dodgy, I don't know. I want to be careful what I'm walking into. Best do that in a pair.'

'Of course,' said Ross. 'You could always bring down the boss.'

'She's the boss for the reason, Ross. She needs to be there. It's up to me to investigate. Once we find something, we'll bring her down. How fast do you think you can get to Aviemore?'

'Forty minutes. Something like that,' he said.

'Fine. You can pick me up in the tea shop just as you come off to the left of the A9 up across the track.'

'Will do.'

'Oh, and Ross?'

'Yes.'

'For that quip about Frank, you're paying!'

She gave a quick smile as she closed down the phone call, and then explained to Anna Clark she'd need to go. Once she'd stepped back outside, Clarissa got into her car and headed for the little coffee shop. She was hungry, but she'd found something out. Step by step, that's how you did this job, little by little, and it felt like it. She sat behind the wheel. She suddenly saw the image of Frank before her and part of her just wanted this investigation done.

Blimey, Clarissa, she said to herself, *you've got it bad this time*. Then she smiled. *And it's blooming great.*

Chapter 10

It took Ross about forty minutes to drive to the small café that Clarissa was sitting in. She had devoured a scone and a large cup of coffee, blaming it entirely on being fed tea instead of a decent cup. She just wanted time out. Things have been moving on in her private life, and she wasn't getting time to reflect on them. All she wanted was to wallow in them. The early stages of a relationship were always exciting, and she wasn't one to fret about it and whether it would go this way or that. Rather, she was the one to enjoy the moment. Because of this, she didn't spot Ross as he marched into the café and then tapped her on the shoulder.

'You doing the *Times* crossword in your head or something?' he said. 'Come on, you're the one called me down.'

She stood up and looked at him almost indignantly. 'Als, sometimes you've just got to let a woman be a woman.' She stood and marched past him. He wouldn't have a clue, she thought. *None of them would have a clue. They weren't old enough. They weren't at that point when the third, fourth, and fifth chances had gone by, but this was real. The only one that would understand, possibly, would've been Seoras, she thought. Seoras. I am not confiding in Seoras about it.*

'I thought we'd take my car,' said Ross.

'No,' came the answer, and Clarissa jumped into the little green sports car. 'If you're going to do this job, Als, learn to do it in style.'

'When I make sergeant, I'm not taking this,' he said.

'When you make sergeant, I'll be an inspector. There's no need to look at me with those eyes.'

'You're too rough to make it as an inspector,' said Ross, and then suddenly went red, realising he said it out loud.

'I remember the old days when your sergeant would've slapped you for that one.' Instead, she started the car and spun it out of the car park. She almost laughed at seeing Ross's face.

Feshiebridge was not a large place, comprising a few houses, but finding the correct one took almost ten minutes. The other houses they went to had pointed out to a little cottage, slightly separate from everyone else. When they asked who lived there, they said, 'Sam.' They thought he was a foreigner. He said little to anyone. He didn't come out much, and nobody knew what he did for a living.

The old green sports car trundled up a muddy drive towards a cottage sitting on the edge of a field. To one side was the start of a small wood, and exiting the car, Clarissa looked but could not see anyone around. She marched up to the front door.

'Do you want me to take the back?' asked Ross. 'In case we've a runner.'

'What makes you think he's going to run? All we've got is a phone number. You've got a very suspicious mind,' said Clarissa.

'I am a detective,' said Ross.

Clarissa wandered across the front of the house. Around the side, she peered in the windows, but she could see no movement. No lights were on and the curtains were not closed.

'I'm not sure there's anyone in,' she said, and walked up and rapped on the door. No one answered. 'I'm not seeing anyone, Als.' She wondered where he'd gone. He'd been round the back of the house, and she'd heard him continue to walk, but he hadn't appeared at the front. Then there came a clucking and several chickens seemed to shout their annoyance at someone. She left the front door, walked to the side of the house, well away from the main building. There was a small coop, and she could see Ross on his knees peering at a water station.

'What are you doing down there?' she asked.

'The water's cold,' he said. 'This is fresh.'

'How do you know it's fresh if it's cold? I mean, it's cold out here.'

'No, it's tap cold. If this water has been out for a while, it'll be at a temperature around us, and we're in summer, so it's not cold. Water doesn't come out of the tap at fifteen or sixteen degrees. It comes out cooler than that because the pipes are underneath and this is like it's come out of a tap.'

She watched as he opened the front of the coop and looked inside. Quickly, he withdrew his head as there was a cluck, a fluff of feathers, and a rather annoyed hen seemed to almost shuffle her back side at him before racing off.

'Would you leave the farm life alone,' said Clarissa, but Ross was reaching for something.

'Food's fresh. It's not been interfered with at all.'

'What do you mean by that?'

'If you put the food out, the chickens will come and investigate it, even if they're not hungry. They'll stick in their head, and then they'll push it about. This is flat, like somebody's shaken it and put it down.'

'When did you learn about this?'

'Brother's a farmer; got a smallholding with a few chickens.'

'Let's try the house again,' said Clarissa. She marched back and rapped on the door again. This time, she hit it with her fist. The door swung open. 'Ross, over here,' she said quickly.

Ross walked up behind her and followed Clarissa inside the house. It was quaint but almost had a seventies' feel to it. Every bit of furniture looked old. Colours that were the thing people threw out to the charity shop because it was so kitsch, so from long ago. Maybe one of those posh charity shops would sell it to you. Everybody was going retro in the house, but for most people, this stuff was just too old, too out of style.

'No photos,' said Ross. 'There are no photos anywhere. How does that work?'

'Somebody that's not staying.'

Ross turned and looked at her. 'Well, clearly he's not staying. He's not here.'

Clarissa marched past him and looked out the rear window. She took her thumb, licked it, and pretended to wipe something on the window, but she was staring at the wooded patch beyond.

'Als, I want you to go out through the front door. I want you to go wide, really wide, but I want you to end up at the far end of that wood. I'll give you about four minutes.'

'Of course. The reason I'm doing this has got nothing to do with your fitness level or ability to climb over fences and all the other nonsense that's in the way, is it?'

'No,' said Clarissa. 'It's because I'm in charge.' She turned and gave him a cheeky smile.

85

Clarissa could see someone out there, but it was hard to pick out the exact shape. Normally, against such a dark background, you could pick out a Scottish figure. The white of the skin, especially with the face, stuck out, and during a summer like this, most people had a t-shirt on, possibly shorts. *The legs would show unless*, she thought, *they said he was foreign; they did say he was a different skin colour.* She walked over to the sink, picked up a cup, and let the water flow into it. She took a large swig of it, making sure that the figure out there kept its eyes on her.

She held open a few cupboards while staring out the back of the house. Clarissa picked up many random items in the kitchen, studying them as if they were the most important thing in the world. Still, the figure was there. She could see in the distance Ross working hard to come in behind the wood. As she saw him reach it and stride through it, she walked out of the rear door of the house. She had to unlock it, but the key was on the inside, another sign that the owner was probably there in the trees and not gone out for a while.

After opening the back door, Clarissa walked directly towards the wood, her eyes focused on the individual. As she got closer, he realised she was coming straight to him, and he turned and ran. Clarissa didn't. She continued to walk at a fast pace and reached the wood as she heard the first shout. Ross must have been seen. He could take on Ross or the older woman at the front. Which one would you pick? He'd run towards the woman. *Idiot*, she thought. *What an idiot.*

She heard the footsteps come close. It was a simple matter of sticking her leg out. He caught it, just below the knee. He managed two more steps before he hit the ground hard, rolled, and hit a tree. Before he could get up, Clarissa was there with her boot on his throat.

'I'm Detective Sergeant Clarissa Urquhart, and I'm trying to find Samuel Benoît. Are you him?'

The man blurted something, but it was a language that Clarissa didn't recognise.

'I said, are you him? Are you Samuel, Samuel Benoît?' The man again seemed to shake.

'May I suggest, sergeant, that you remove your foot from him, and I'll hold him. At the moment, we've got an ethnic man underneath the foot of a white sergeant. It's probably not the best look, even if he ran.'

'I'm a woman about to hit her sixties,' said Clarissa. 'I am not just a white sergeant.'

'With all due respect,' said Ross, 'When they call you Rottweiler.'

'Stop there,' she said, 'and pick him up.' Clarissa removed her foot. 'Let's go over to the house. I'm not sitting having a chat here in the trees.' As Ross picked him up, he began asking him, 'Are you Samuel? Tell me, who's Samuel Benoît?' but in French. Clarissa could do that; she could do French. In the art world, you had to know your French. Ross being Ross was impeccable with the accent, something that Clarissa struggled with.

Just as they reached the house, they could hear a loud car engine approaching. Clarissa held her hand up, and the small party of three stopped and look towards the drive. A large black van raced down it, and Clarissa waved her hand, showing Ross should get the supposed Mr Benoît inside. She heard him open the door, heard the two men go, but her eyes were focused on the arrival of the van. It spun to a halt, and the side door was opened.

It was black, similar to the van that appeared on live TV to capture Hugh Barkley. From inside, two figures half popped out of the van. They seemed strong. Working together, they were holding a sack, and they give it two swings. Then it was tossed into the driveway. As Clarissa ran towards them, the door of the van was shut, and it sped off.

The bag was long, probably about a person wide. Her heart thumped. Black van arriving at the house of a strange phone number. It wouldn't be good. She looked again at the bag; definitely big enough for a person. At the top, it was tied tight with a plastic cord. It wasn't a body bag, not like the force used, not like the one you would take to the mortuary.

This was just a crude black bag. She fell on her knees, pulling at it. The bag was thick, but it wasn't unsurmountable. As soon as she'd broken a small hole in the bag, the smell of faeces hit her nose straight away and she recoiled, coughing. She fought her way back to it, pulling at the bag, tearing it open.

Inside was the back of a man's head. The body wasn't covered, except in the faeces. It was facedown, and she continued to rip the bag down and found bare buttocks, the colouration of which didn't seem normal. She reached and tried to spin the person over.

He could be alive. She had to check, had to know. Clarissa was waving one hand frantically in the air as she reached down and grabbed the body with the other. She didn't know what her fingers were touching. It was soft, the feel of a chocolate brownie, but the smell, oh the smell was gross. Dog poo!

She pulled down into the bag again, desperate to turn the man over. Letting go of her nose, she tried not to breathe as she grabbed the man's arm and spun him, but the entire bag was still attached. All she ended up with was putting his bare side on the ground.

Clarissa reached down, pulling at the bag desperately. The legs seemed to buckle, and then the bag gave way, ripping at the bottom and she pulled it hard. As she did so, her eyes swept along it. Clarissa dropped the bag and only just turned away in time before she vomited heavily on the floor.

She heard Ross arriving behind her, racing as hard as he could, and then a cry of, 'Oh dear God.' There was a second pair of feet coming too. She heard Ross turning, telling someone to get back, first in English, then in French, then in other languages she didn't know. She looked over at the man they'd apprehended. His eyes were wide, and tears were running down his face. He began shrieking, trying to race forward as Ross held him back.

'Ambulance, boss, ambulance,' he shouted at Clarissa. She reached for her phone deep within the shawl, picked it up, and pressed 999. She couldn't look back because she wouldn't function. The call got put through, and Clarissa gave the details of where they were. When the ambulance operator hung up, she pressed another button and the desk sergeant at the station answered. Once again, her words spat out like a metronome. So solidly rhythmic was her deliverance that every emotion in her voice was taken out. Only once that call had been placed that she turned and looked back at the figure she'd unveiled.

The head was there, the chest too, the legs and the top of the thighs down were also there. But the midriff, dear God the midriff, it was a mass of blood and things were missing. She turned away and vomited again. As she wiped her mouth clean, she looked over and saw Ross fighting with the man. He was still trying to get closer.

'Get him in the house,' said Clarissa. 'Into the house!'

She saw Ross take out handcuffs, manhandle the man's arms, and drag him back to the house. Samuel Benoît cried the whole way, half screaming. Clarissa turned back.

She had to check, had to look one more time. She got down on her knees and looked for a heartbeat. Clarissa checked for breathing. She sought a pulse. When she believed there was nothing there, she stepped back, tears were streaming down her face. Her heart was thumping. Her mouth tasted sick. Sometimes in your life images stay with you. She knew in the police force some officers were haunted by them. She believed this would be one for her.

Chapter 11

Macleod could feel the beads of sweat coming across his forehead. He stared out at the crowd of reporters, many of whom he could name, and most he didn't like. Since his progression to DCI, he had to take more and more of these press conferences. As the senior figure in the department, no longer could he bump the run-of-the-mill ones upstairs because he was upstairs. Neither could he simply just leave them to Hope.

As a DI, there would be an expectation that she would appear on the platform beside him. However, in his time as DI, he changed that perception, offering Hope as his DS to do a major part of the briefing while as DCI he sat there with her. She was a better face for the public. Nobody would have grabbed Macleod and put him on a poster campaign. If there was one thing he was certain of, if somebody was asking him to do something within the department, it wasn't for a public relations effort. Either he was being passed something he didn't want, or they thought he could do the job. At the moment, he really didn't want this job.

'Is this attack against the Church, Detective Chief Inspector?'

Macleod's eyes shot across and spotted Andy Patrick. The

man was a pain, a complete pain, for he whipped things up. He would write whatever story he was going to write, anyway. Macleod never understood his reason for turning up at press conferences, other than to see if Macleod would fall apart.

'Investigations are continuing, although clearly the victims so far have indeed been Church members.'

'Does that mean then these attacks are being carried against Church members?'

'Because we can only go off the attacks that have happened, and rather than anything that's going to happen in the future, if indeed there are any more planned, then yes, I thought that was quite self-evident.'

Somebody would probably chin him for that last bit, but Macleod didn't care. It was a stupid question. They were trying to get him to say these were attacks against the Church, which anybody looking at them could rightly say. After all, the pair were both ministers. And this, thought Macleod, is a waste of time.

The team was waiting to be briefed. Hope would have pulled them in, got them ready to assemble as soon as Macleod came back off the press conference. He didn't want her disturbed, especially since Clarissa was struggling. He didn't blame her. Few people saw a sight like that. Jona would also be back with her conclusions from the death and hopefully some answers about the DNA from the hair that Sarah Melbourne had grabbed.

In front of him, more hands were going up. Macleod wasn't watching them. He was thinking. Derek Clark had been in a sham marriage. He'd been killed with serious damage being done to his nether reasons. Barkley had died in a highly sexualized manner, but not in a manner that had any sort of love behind it. There must have been abuse in the background, but how did they connect both ministers? Was it just a wide attack on the Church?

He hoped not, because that would make it almost impossible to predict who would be attacked next. There was also a team of people behind it, four people on each snatch, and some of them women. He was of that age that he still found it repugnant that a woman could be involved in such a murder. Of course, he knew it was more than possible.

He'd seen so much in his time, but back in his day, women's role in society was very different. Might have been wrong, and he was the first nowadays to say that a strong, confident woman like Hope was better than the shy and retiring partner his own wife had been. His current partner, Jane, got afforded so much more. Society had changed for the better. Maybe we weren't all there yet. He certainly wasn't.

Macleod heard another question. This one was fielded by the Assistant Chief Constable. The murders were taking a national bent. Although both of them were in the northern part of Scotland, the media interest was picking up. They were always interested, but then they became like hounds. Next, all the stories got twisted, and you had to be careful that you didn't get involved in what was a fantasy as opposed to the proper investigation.

'I think if there's no more questions for DCI Macleod, we should let him go. He's got a murderer to catch. I'll remain here and answer any other questions you may have.'

Macleod looked over at Jim and did his best not to mouth, 'Thank you.' He stood up, turned, walked off the platform, and disappeared back into the recesses of the police station. Two flights of steps later, he was walking into the main office, the one that used to be attached to his own side office. He missed it, being able to watch the team.

'Good,' said Hope as he walked in. 'Now that the DCI's here, we'll begin.' Macleod shuffled off to one side, giving Hope the floor, and was suddenly presented with a cup of coffee by Ross. He gave his thanks and turned to listen to what Hope would say.

'Two dead ministers,' said Hope. 'Both of them killed in a fashion that indicates some sort of sexual abuse that has happened in the past. One was preceded by a greetings card to a police officer, and that one doesn't quite make sense,' said Hope. 'Why? Why contact Angus McNeil, a former policeman based mainly on the Isle of Lewis? Why not contact him with the second one? What are we missing?

'In both cases, our subjects were jumped and taken away in a van to be abused in whatever fashion and killed. It's looking at the moment like it could be the same four people that did the abductions. However, we have very little detail on them. The van's been burnt out. Second van's not been found. Let's get up to speed with where we're at. Ross,' said Hope.

'Well, update just in, Inspector. The second van's been found burned out. Forensics aren't getting anything from it. Said it's well destroyed. We've checked through any link from Angus McNeil, who received the card, to one of our victims, Hugh Barkley. Nothing so far. In terms of their churches and their church life, I can't connect Derek Clark to Hugh Barkley in any shape, sense, or form. Not even meeting at conferences. Certainly, never shared a church floor together.'

'Do we think it's random, then?'

'No,' said Macleod. 'It's not random. Something's afoot. Somebody doing something random wouldn't have bothered with the letter. You've got to know when you send the card to Angus McNeil, he's going to talk to me. He was my boss back in the day. Whoever's committed these murders must know that we were going to be put on the situation. Therefore, they're playing something, but I don't know what. Sorry, you can continue, Ross.'

Ross gave Macleod a slight nod, then turned and said, 'The area where they were abducted or the bodies were dumped has no CCTV. We got the camera footage from the TV company, but it's telling us very little.'

'What about purchases of vans?' asked Hope.

'Nothing. Checking through where those types of vans have been purchased, but we're talking too many people. Even if we've tracked down that van and it's a very popular van,' said Ross, 'we're going to be looking at eighty people. That's if they're buying them and not just stealing them.'

'Have we had any reports of theft?'

'One,' said Ross. 'But it's so far away. Hard to put a definite link on it. I've got forensics checking the numbers on the frames of the vehicles. That's if they're still intact.'

'What about relatives?' asked Hope to Clarissa. For a moment, the sergeant didn't look up, but then she seemed to take a deep breath before saying, 'We have a sham marriage between Anna and Derek. Hugh Barkley is on his own. Finding very little from the families.'

'Anything from forensics, Jona?' asked Hope.

'Well, as we know, Reverent Hugh Barkley was raped, and he also was abused with sexual implements, causing him to suffocate. Possibly the use of over-sized or exaggerated implements,' said Jona. 'I can give you more detail if you wish, but I think you gather what I'm talking about.'

'And it was shoved down his throat,' stated Hope.

'Repeatedly,' said Jona, 'and then eventually held there. It blocked the passageway, and he couldn't breathe and suffocated.'

'Okay,' said Hope, 'and what about Derek Clark?'

'Derek Clark, I believe, was abused similarly except that when he died, it was because of massive blood loss with all of his sexual organs at the front removed.'

'In what way removed?' asked Macleod.

'Cut off, thereby causing massive blood loss. He was then put inside the bag and inside the bag was dumped lots and lots of dog faeces. Seems to be a second dose in the same place. It doesn't look like they went back to a second kennels.'

Clarissa stood up suddenly and ran from the room.

'Hope,' said Macleod, 'just go check. We'll wait.'

Hope left the room and there was a slight murmur going around before Macleod stood up. 'Listen,' he said, 'this is a tough one. Some of us can deal with seeing stuff like this, but, when it's just put in front of you, well, sometimes it gets to you, okay? So, let's cut the Sergeant some slack. She's going to need it and I'm going to need her.'

'Of course,' said Ross, 'I think I go for everyone here in saying that we all have a great respect for her.'

'I don't need the speech, Ross, as good of you as it is to do it. We just need to cut a bit of slack to everyone because this might not be the last body we see.'

'Are you sure there's going to be more?' asked a constable.

'I'll not say anything further until the Inspector returns and the Sergeant, but, know this, you're probably not going to get a lot of home time in the next week or two.'

It took five minutes before Clarissa walked in looking white and a bit embarrassed. Macleod approached Hope as she came back in, and she simply gave a nod and said that Clarissa was okay.

'Is that you finished, Jona?' asked Hope.

'No. We checked the DNA from the hair that was grabbed by Sarah Melbourne. Seems we have no match for it and we could be looking at somebody who's never killed before.'

'And in a large group,' said Macleod.

'Looks like we're going to have to be doing a lot more legwork,' said Hope. 'We need to make some connections between our deceased and our recipient of the cards.'

'I've gone through all the computer records; we're not finding anything.'

'Well, then dig further, Ross,' said Hope suddenly. She saw Ross's rather annoyed-looking face. 'We're getting panned by the press out there. We need to make something happen.'

'But I can't just make something happen,' said Ross. 'We're going through the work. We've got people out there asking questions.'

'Well, get them to ask more,' said Hope. She looked under stress, but Macleod said nothing.

'Well, that's about it, unless you have something to say, Chief Inspector?'

'I do, Hope, I do.' He stood up and walked to the front. 'Take a seat, please,' he said to Hope.

'Hope's not wrong. These things are getting bigger. The press is onto us more, so I'm growing the team. I'm going to take charge and run the investigation. This is not a slight on Hope, it's just the case has got a lot bigger, and I need her where she's going to be most effective. We're going to run two teams with me at the top. One of those teams will be led by Hope.

You're tasked with looking into those who have been killed, pooling together any similarities. Go through the families, go through where they've been, get into their history. Clarissa?'

Clarissa looked up, still incredibly pale. 'I want you to look at the letter that came through. There's got to be a connection there. I know, Angus. He came straight to me. Somebody is playing us. Somebody wants to make sure that there's a message being held up. I don't know what it is at the moment, it's not clear. You're on that side.

'Both of you will use Ross and his team and whoever else we bring in. I'm going to haul in a couple of extra higher-up detectives. You three have been great, but I think we need a few more of our own helping us out. However, in the meantime, Ross, I want a trawl of historical abuse cases. I want anything that fits what happened to these Ministers. They're killed in a certain way. I want to know how, why, what does it match up with? Bring me sheets. If there are a lot of matches, bring them up and we'll chase through all of them, but that's your job.

'I'll get extra people in tomorrow. Until then, work with what you've got, but you pull on any lead. You pull on anything and you match up anything. If there's a vague connection, I want to know about it. Our press will see the team is expanded. That's fine. It's just routine. It's a bigger operation, it's widespread, blame it on the geography if anyone asks. Anything beyond that they want, fire it to me. We need to get on top of this one, and quick. I have a feeling we haven't seen the last here. We have four people conducting the kidnap. Maybe we've got a team of abused people, maybe there's more people out there to have retribution visited upon. But we don't need this going out of control! Does everyone understand?'

There were various nods, and Macleod gave a faint smile. 'We'll get there. We'll get this lot, don't worry about that. This is the usual starting point, very hard to see anything, but I think we're looking for several people, several connected people. We need to join the dots, and fast. Everyone, heads down and get on with it. Hope, Clarissa, with me.'

He turned and walked towards the small office beside the main one and was about to step through the door when he stopped. Hope and Clarissa approached him.

'Do you mind if we use your office?' he said to Hope. She gave a faint smile, nodded, and Macleod led her in through the office first.

'Do you want to take the big seat?' said Hope, pointing to the desk and the large chair behind it. It was the one that had been Macleod's for many years, the one he'd vacated for her.

'No,' he said, 'let's sit at the round table.'

The round table was as described and could fit about five people around it. Macleod had used it for small meetings previously and Hope had left it there.

'It's better if we use that. Let them see that this is your office because it is. I'm not taking this investigation from you because you've done anything wrong. It's just got bigger and needs a bigger task force, okay?'

She looked down at him and Macleod could see in her eyes, she was hurting. She hadn't been an inspector that long.

'You know I trust you,' he said. 'This isn't about whether you can do the job. Between the three of us, this is going to be tough. We're going to get hauled over the coals because we may not pull them all in quick enough. There's going to be more deaths. That's why I'm running it. I need you both out there. I need you both doing what you do best and, as for you,' he said, turning to Clarissa, 'don't worry about being sick. Don't worry about struggling with what we see. If you need help, take it. Go talk to the counsellors, whatever, but I need my Rottweiler. We're going to have to kick people for this.'

He smiled as she gave a grin, too. 'Okay,' she said.

'I need a word with Hope,' said Macleod. 'If you give us a minute?'

'Of course,' said Clarissa.

But, as she reached the door, Macleod shouted out to her again, 'Clarissa, you can't tell him. You can't share that one with him, not now. Not really when it's over, they don't need to know. It's bad if they know it to that extent. Just say you saw something bad, don't explain it. He might not handle it. I'm not sure Jane could. If you need to talk, we're here.'

'Yes, we are,' said Hope. Clarissa gave a nod and then left, closing the door behind her.

'What else did you have to say?' she asked.

'I need you to monitor this. They've come to Angus McNeil and then to me. There may be a link to me, there may be something I don't want to produce from the past. I can't think what it is, but it's been a long past. Keep me honest.' He looked at Hope's rather surprised face.

'Keep you honest,' she said. 'When are you not honest?'

'We all make mistakes. They're all there. I was never perfect, far from it. But when the pressure is on, you never know what you'll cover up, what you'll keep from yourself. Keep me honest.' He watched her face, almost struggling to comprehend what she was hearing. 'I know you will.'

With that, he turned and opened the door. 'I'll be upstairs if there're anymore developments.'

Macleod left, taking the stairs up to his own office. He wasn't sure there was something, but those earlier days, they were different, especially under Angus McNeil's tutelage. Things were different.

Chapter 12

Eileen Beaton was hacked off ever since her legs had failed to work and her hands had become unsteady. She had felt part of her had died. Her husband had died many years before and so Eileen now lived in a care home of sorts. She had her own flat. Well, flatlet, she liked to say, because it wasn't big. There was a bedroom, a small lounge, a kitchenette, but she could also take herself for meals, along with everyone else in the care facility in the small dining area.

She had help come in every day as well. She was thankful for the pension she had earned, which allowed her to have this level of care. Life was okay. She got out and about. Usually with taxis, and being pushed here or there, but it was manageable. Others she knew had not been so fortunate.

Today she'd been out for dinner only with the bowling club. She'd used to play, but now she just went along to watch as much for the entertainment and laughter as to enjoying the bowling. It had been something to get her out when she'd retired. Peterhead wasn't a terrible place to live. She'd found plenty to do, plenty of views off the coast as well. It was funny how an afternoon could be enjoyed just sitting in the chair, watching what was going on around you. Wildlife, animals, clouds on the move.

The taxi driver had opened the door and Eileen had wheeled herself in. The post was sitting up on the table, left up there by the care home staff. It always came through and dropped to the floor, and wasn't easy for Eileen to collect it. The table was a better height than the floor.

Before she would sit and read it, she wheeled herself to her bedroom, took off her jacket, and laid it out on the bed, wheeling herself back in. She used a low-set kettle and reached for a mug to make herself some coffee.

She glanced over at the envelopes. Bill, bill, something, and her National Trust renewal. Maybe they'd sent out the card. She ripped that one open first, found the new card inside and carefully detached it before putting it away inside her purse.

She then looked at the first bill, electric, more than usual. Although she paid for the care in the little flat that she was in, the building was bought outright, and so she covered her own bills. It was a rather unique arrangement, but one that suited her, for it made her feel more independent.

The second bill backed that up. Gas. Going up as ever. Eileen put them both to one side before looking at the envelope before her. It was plain brown. The handwriting was rather poor. In some ways, it was like a scrawl, except Eileen thought it was done by somebody using the wrong hand. The letters were so poorly formed, yet just about readable. It was certainly nobody's handwriting she knew.

She tore the top of the envelope open and found a card inside. She pulled it out quickly before turning it round. There was a torso with a backside. She wasn't sure if it was male or female, androgynous in its shape. Across both the torso and the bare behind were large marks, like somebody had whipped them.

She held the card in front of her hand, staring at it. Then slowly she opened it. There was nothing else inside. She flipped it over to the back. Again, nothing. Just the image on the front. She stared at it again. Then she pressed the red button that called for help. Part of her was trembling. Part of her was almost unsure of what to do.

'Eileen, what's the matter, love?'

It was Brenda dressed in her green outfit. Eileen thought they all looked too much like paramedics. She would have given them more of a hotel staff look. But she was in care of some sort.

'I just received this,' she said to Brenda and handed her the card. As Brenda went to grab it, Eileen suddenly snatched it back and placed it on the table.

'What's the matter?' asked Brenda.

'Don't touch it. There might be fingerprints on it. We shouldn't contaminate it anymore.'

'What do you mean?' asked Brenda. She walked forward, looking down at it. 'All right,' she said. 'What? Who sent you that? It's rude, isn't it?'

'It's not rude. Sadistic,' said Eileen. 'Look at it. Those are whip marks across the back and across the buttocks. Who would seriously do that? Why send me the card?'

'Must have been something from your past. You were in the police force. Some people will never get over you. Some people always want to keep getting back at you,' said Brenda. 'I'll put it in the bin.'

'No,' said Eileen. 'Can you reach me the phone?'

'The phone? You're not going to call the police, are you?'

'I'm just going to do some checking,' she said. 'A friend of mine, well, an old colleague, McNeil, he received a card. I heard it on the grapevine talking to somebody from the old school. I'm just worried some other people might have got some. Can you get me my phone book?' Eileen didn't like modern mobile phones. Besides, the phone book went back much further.

'Are you okay?' asked Brenda, handing the phonebook back over. 'Are you…'

'I'm all right,' said Eileen. 'Just a wee bit. Well, a wee bit taken aback, I guess. Can you put the kettle on?'

Brenda reached forward, pressed the button, and realised that the kettle was already warm. 'You've already done it, Eileen. I'll pour you something, shall I?'

'Please do,' she said. She placed several phone calls in the next half an hour. Out of the six people she phoned, she got one positive response. Former DCI Anthony Henderson had apparently received a rather disgusting card. His daughter had been informed about it, but the staff had put the letter into the bin. As Eileen was talking to the daughter, she could feel herself shivering. Her eyes glanced back towards the card with the whip marks. She had to make another call.

She hadn't spoken to this man in years, and yet she always remembered him. Nowadays, his face was often on the television. He had done well for himself, but he still had that rather dour demeanour, that seriousness. She never liked the church. Never been that fond of many people in it. When she'd worked up on Lewis, he had been so derogatory in how he spoke to her. Wasn't a woman's job to be in there, jobs for the boys, it should have been. Mans work, the police force. There he was these days, that Hope McGrath working for him, and apparently, he got Urquhart as well. She wondered how they stomached him.

'DCI Macleod,' came the voice on the other end. 'DCI, this is Eileen Beaton,' she said. 'You might not remember me, we were in…'

'Stornoway,' said Macleod on the other end. 'We were in Stornoway; you were working in the office.'

'That's correct,' she said, but she couldn't say much more.

'Must be quite hard for you to call me. I can't imagine I'm someone you want to speak to.'

'Indeed not, Inspector.'

'Call me Seoras, if you can,' he said. 'I'm a bit different from how I used to be.'

'You were very oppressive; took nothing I said seriously. You thought very little of me, didn't you?'

'I thought very little of many people, especially people outside of, well, who didn't live life the way I thought it should be led. You drank quite a bit in those days, Eileen, and I punished you for it. I must have been- how do people put it? A pompous git.'

'Fucking arsehole,' said Eileen. 'That's what you were.'

'Probably right. No,' said Macleod. 'No, probably about it. I apologise. I wasn't good back then. Thought I was, but I wasn't, and the way I dealt with women was bad. I'm sorry.'

Eileen felt a lump in her throat, struggled and had to check back some tears that were forming. She hadn't expected this, she hadn't expected that he would realise how he had behaved to her all those years ago.

'Are you okay?' asked Macleod. 'But I guess you're not calling me because you wanted to talk to an old idiot like me. You must have been calling for a reason.'

'I was,' she said, 'I was. You're quite good at what you do, aren't you? I've seen you on the telly. You've solved a few things.'

'That was never a problem,' said Macleod. 'I could always get to the bottom of stuff; I just wasn't good with people. Just wasn't, well, you know.'

'I got sent a card,' said Eileen. 'It's got a torso on it, with whipped marks across it. Stripes, as you would say. Proper bloodied stripes.'

'I received another one,' said Macleod, 'Angus McNeil, but he got a letter detailing sexual abuse and the death of a minister, and then we had a minister that died that way.'

'Have you had any more ministers die? There was something on the news.'

'Yes, there was,' said Macleod. 'But we kept the most of it out of the press. You don't want them detailing things.'

'Did they take away everything?' asked Eileen. 'I mean, did they cut it all off?'

'Explain,' said Macleod quickly.

'The genitals, his man bits. Did they?'

'How did you know that?' asked Macleod. 'Did you get a previous card?'

'No,' she said. 'Anthony Henderson, he's gone a bit, well, senile. He's got dementia. The staff threw the card out, but apparently, it was a 3D one. It was of two men, but one chopped off parts of the other man.'

'Which home?' asked Macleod excitedly. 'Which home?'

'It's down in Oban. I guess we're going to be on the phone for a while.'

* * *

Ellie Fraser raised her hands and committed the meeting to

the Lord. There weren't many of them, a mere six in the house church, but that wasn't the point. Where a few were gathered, there the Lord was also. She pulled the curtains. Despite what one member had said about being visible, they were there to pray and to talk, and to share. Not there for public display. Besides, young Steven was with them tonight, only Fourteen. She'd have to make sure some of the older ones didn't go off on too much of a tangent; didn't bore the poor lad to death.

After she'd prayed, she sat down and took out her Bible, and read to the group. The passage tonight was about Peter and how he made the change to accepting the Gentiles. He'd done away with the food rules, the ones that had blocked others coming to the church. She always hated that. But since her early, wilder years, she had found something. Who'd have thought it, that when she'd stepped out to find somewhere to hide, instead she would find something that made her life?

The thing was, she had plenty to repent of, from those earlier days, days when she didn't know what she was doing. At least, that's what she constantly told herself. Days when God didn't matter. *Just read it, read it and get the discussion going. That's when things happened. That's when he spoke to people.* That's when the doorbell went.

'You keep reading, Ellie,' said Steven. 'I can get the door for you.'

'Thank you,' said Ellie, and continued to read the passage in front of her. As the others sat listening to her, Ellie heard a commotion at the door, then feet were thumping. The door to her living room was pushed open. Someone had Steven at knifepoint. The person was masked and dressed in black, and three others burst in behind her.

Jim, the sixty-year-old deacon of the church, stepped forward, keen to step in and help, but he was hit and hit hard. The piece of wood struck him on the face. Blood exploded from his nose, and he fell backwards. Steven was thrown to one side as the person with the knife came at Ellie. She raised her hands, unable to move, unable to run.

'Don't hurt them,' said Ellie. 'Don't hurt them!' Someone picked up a chair and Ellie saw a young woman being thrown against the wall. Somebody put a hood over her, and she was dragged kicking and screaming from the room. She twisted and turned as best she could, but there was no escaping the powerful arms that had her. Maybe she should relax, maybe be quiet, maybe try to take in what was happening. Try to remember voices, but suddenly there weren't any. All was quiet. She was picked up, and then she, too, was thrown. Her shoulder hurt as it hit the bottom of what she thought was a metallic floor.

She rolled and then was hauled upright, sitting on her bottom. The hood was lifted slightly, and a gag was tied around her mouth before the hood was put back down. She then heard people get out and the sliding of a van door before it sped off. It had been quick, less than two minutes from Steven answering the door. She felt herself tip this way and that as the van raced around corners before settling down into a more steady pace. Then someone lifted the hood up.

Ellie's eyes took a moment to adjust. It took her time to realise that the person in front of her wasn't holding a knife and wasn't threatening her. Instead, he was smiling. It was Steven. Steven was in the van with her.

She tried to speak, but she couldn't say anything, and it took a moment for Steven to pull the gag down.

'What are you doing?' she asked. 'Where are we?'

'It's okay,' said Steven. 'We're in a van. They've taken you in a van, but I'm here.'

Ellie tried to look around in the darkness but could see so very little. She'd been snatched by four people and taken away in a van. They had hit people in her congregation. Jim had a smashed nose, Andrea thrown against the wall, and now here she was with her Steven. Ellie knew she was in trouble, but dear God, why was this boy with her?

Chapter 13

The chippy light green sports car of Clarissa Urquhart raced along a rather damp road towards Peterhead. News had come in of another kidnapping. The pressure was on. She had grabbed her new start that morning before he'd had a chance to even acquaint himself with the rest of the team. Detective Constable Eric Patterson was a name Clarissa had heard of, an up-and-coming officer. Yet, when she found him that morning, she was rather distressed to see he was from the cookie-cutter mould.

His suit was snappy, but not too much. The hair was neatly parted on the left-hand side and then swept across, held by what she thought must have been a massive amount of gel. His shoes were crisp and clean, and even the crease in his trousers was ironed to perfection.

Conversely, Clarissa hadn't got into trews this morning, but was in her jeans with a trademark shawl wrapped around her. She'd find that since she joined the murder squad, slowly her sense of style had been eroded, or rather, put on the back burner. Long nights and the lack of sleep meant she didn't spend as much time picking out what she wanted to wear.

Not that she'd been home for that long. In the hour and a

half she'd been there, Frank had popped round. It was five-thirty in the morning and she had texted him to say that she wouldn't be able to see him over the next few days because of the case. Her head was still spinning from having seen what remained of Derek Clark. In a lot of ways, she was worried about seeing Frank.

When he rang the doorbell, she had wondered who it would be. On opening, she felt elation seeing the man that she was falling for, but then she just burst into tears. In shock, he stood there while she held on to him on the doorstep, weeping into his shoulder. After a few minutes, he had coaxed her to the sofa.

Then he'd asked what was wrong, and she said she couldn't tell him.

'Nothing about it?' he'd asked. 'You can tell me nothing about it?'

'No,' she'd said. She'd gone for a shower, trying to clean up after explaining to him she was on the road for Peterhead. He made her coffee and breakfast. It was only when she left she realised she hadn't asked him anything about him. *Was he all right? What had happened over at the club?*

She'd seen the concern in his eyes when she left, but hoped that it wasn't putting him off. Police officers, especially those in the murder squad, were often hard to live with. You try not to bring your work home with you, but some of it just stayed.

Clarissa looked up. The lorry was going too slow, so she dropped a gear, and pulled out in the little green sports car. She whipped around the front and back in lane just before a car came around the corner ahead.

'Do you not think that was a bit tight?' asked DC Patterson beside her. He had his hand up on the dash in front of him and seemed to be braced for an impact. Clarissa didn't understand what he was talking about. She could handle this car. This is what she did, but if the guy was going to criticise her driving, he could get out and walk.

'There was loads of room. Just get onto that map. Tell me where I'm going.'

'Of course, but I would appreciate it if you slowed down a touch.'

'We haven't got time to slow down. Someone is missing. We're getting the information to help.'

Then came a cough beside her.

'Don't. All right? If you've got something to say, you just say it,' spat Clarissa.

'I think you should slow down, or maybe I could drive for a bit.'

'No,' said Clarissa. 'Nobody else drives this. Okay? This is my car. Nobody drives my car.'

'You're the senior officer.'

'That's right, I'm the senior officer. Look, Eric, just start thinking about the case. We need a new perspective. You're coming in from the outside, you haven't dealt with it so far. Tell me what you think.'

'Well, clearly there's several people who've got an angst against these ministers.'

'Clearly,' said Clarissa.

'Maybe there's something in the past,' said Eric. 'Maybe there's an event that a church caused, or some sort of abuse ring happening. Those things have happened.'

'I may have used to work for the art division and am now in the murder squad, but I'm not blind or deaf. I have heard of these things.'

'You asked me to.'

'Yes, I did. Ease up, will you? I think that tie's up so tight around your neck, you're going to choke.' She glanced over at the man. He could only have been twenty-five.

'How do you want to play it when we reach the home?' asked Eric.

'I'll take the lead with the questions. If you've got something to ask, not a problem, but don't steal my thunder. Don't jump in front of me. Okay? Don't be afraid to push, she's a former police officer. She's one of ours, so I expect you to ask the hard questions.'

They took another half an hour before they were at the home. Clarissa pulled the sports car right up to the front door.

'Do you think we should park here?' asked Eric.

'I've just driven miles, I'm not walking more miles just to get into that place and yes, I'm on an urgent case. I will park here. Do you think you can actually do something regarding the case and not about me?'

She knew she was being eggy. Well, what did they expect? It had been a rough one. When Frank turned up at the door, and after crying her eyes out, all she'd wanted to do was to sit on the sofa with him. Just lay in his arms, not actually do anything, just have him hold her. Maybe that was a good thing. Maybe it wasn't all about sex and bedroom antics anymore.

Clarissa laughed to herself. It had been a long time since it was all about sex and bedroom antics. Not that those things were off the table anymore, it's just that they were a little more relaxed. Yes, that was a suitable term. Relaxed. She needed a bit more than just that. Besides, with what she'd seen recently, it was difficult to comprehend or think about those sorts of things.

Clarissa sent DC Patterson off to find the manager of the home while she popped off to use the facilities. On return, she found him waiting with the manager. As she approached, he held out his arm and introduced Detective Sergeant Clarissa Urquhart, saying she'd been a longtime stalwart of the force. Clarissa felt she was at a gala dinner being introduced to the queen or something.

'Sergeant Urquhart,' said Clarissa, reaching forward with her hand. 'If we could just see Eileen, we need to be quick about this. It's rather urgent.'

'I've been hearing similar reports. Of course, Eileen's of very sound mind. She had an injury that caused her legs to not work properly. Her hands are also restricted, but her mind is as sharp as ever. I warn you, she may be a little acerbic. It's difficult being stuck like that.'

'She's a policewoman. We're all acerbic,' said Clarissa. 'Now where is she?'

Clarissa thought she heard a tut coming from Patterson, but she ignored it. If he kept it up, she'd soon break him back down. He wouldn't be the first up-and-coming officer that tried to correct her.

Clarissa was shown through to a small room in a flatlet attached to the main complex. Eileen Beaton was sitting in a wheelchair. She had several cups placed in front of her.

'You take coffee?' she asked. 'I take it you're Urquhart.'

'That's me,' said Clarissa, 'but just call me Clarissa. This is Eric Patterson. He'll probably want you to call him DC Patterson, and I hope to God that's coffee. It's been a long drive over.'

Eileen laughed and told Clarissa to take a seat. 'And what about you, DC Patterson?' she asked.

'It's Eric. You can call me Eric.'

'Lucky you,' said Clarissa. She sat in silence as Eileen made up several coffees and then passed them across from her wheelchair.

'I hear you're up against it,' said Eileen.

'Where are you hearing that from?' asked Clarissa.

'The old network. You know how it is, don't you?'

'The details of current cases shouldn't really be…'

'Shut up, Eric,' said Clarissa. 'She's one of us, all right? All right, Eileen, take me through it. What happened?'

'Well, I sent the scan of the card over to Macleod. I used to work with him, you see. I'd heard about a few of the other cards, bits and pieces, and I phoned round after I got my own. That's how I dug up about Anthony's card. I mean, he's not all there, and the staff put it in the bin. I mean, you get a card like that; who the hell puts it in the bin? You'd pass it on, wouldn't you?'

'I'm hoping we're going to get it. I'm afraid the Oban uniform won't be too happy with us. They're checking through the bins at the moment.'

Eileen laughed. 'Oh, you'll be popular. But on this one I got whip marks. The way it was drawn, it was a torso and a pair of buttocks, and you could see the whip marks. But they were done not like stripes on a zebra, but like ingrained stripes. You could see where they'd drawn the blood that comes from the whip mark. I'd say there was a venom behind it. The artistry…'

'What I'm trying to work out, though,' said Clarissa, 'is why you? Why Henderson? Why McNeil?'

'Well, I used to work with McNeil,' she said. 'I was with McNeil up in Stornoway. So was Henderson. Early days. McNeil was older. But we were there. So was Seoras.'

'I knew Seoras was there,' said Clarissa. 'Didn't realise he was there at your time.'

'I didn't really work with him much, but, well, he was very sharp. Really didn't like women. I mean, you were the second-class citizens, if I put it politely.'

'But he'd lost his wife,' said Clarissa. 'That affected him, didn't it?'

'This was before that. His wife was still with him. It was bizarre. I don't think they were that long married. All along, he'd been quite a zealot. Been in the church and, well, I don't know if you know the churches up there. I didn't suit them. Certainly, back in those days. They might have changed now, they might not have, but men were the order of the day. They were first. Women were second. Much more so than on the mainland. Guess that didn't bother someone like yourself, though.'

'What do you mean?' asked Clarissa.

'The Rottweiler. That's what they call you, isn't it? Macleod's Rottweiler. Even before Macleod, you were well known for taking people on. Snapped a few young ones back into place.' Clarissa saw Eileen glance over at Eric and almost gave a little smug laugh.

'How long were you up on Lewis?'

'Three, four years. I was not a proper officer then. Very early days for me, I was a slip of a girl. Really, a glorified secretary. The thing about Macleod was, I used to have to get him his coffee. He always complained.'

'Always the one for the coffee. He's changed, though. His attitude's changed.'

'Well, he apologised to me. Actually, sounded quite shell-shocked when I spoke to him.'

'He's quite the guy now. He's got DI McGrath working with him as well. Today's world's very different.'

'I believe so,' said Eileen. 'I mean, I got up the ranks, but I'm glad I'm out of it. I've seen too many things, and what would I do now except stay behind a desk? With these legs that don't work anymore.'

'Was there anything at the time regarding sexual impropriety in Stornoway?'

Clarissa glanced over at Eric. She'd told him to ask questions, but this came a little out of left field. Not really in the conversation's flow.

'Not a lot that I can remember, but then again, I was only a glorified secretary. I didn't see everything. In those days, records weren't as good. We didn't put everything down, I reckon. Certain things were kept out of the official domain. Having seen the card, I thought about that. There was nothing coming to my mind.'

Clarissa found out a few more details, but nothing of significance. The card was whisked off to forensics, but she hadn't had the discovery she'd hoped. Outside, in the little green sports car, she could see Patterson becoming agitated because she hadn't started the car.

'I'm thinking,' she said. 'Don't do that.'

'Do what?'

'Don't sit there and fidget in the face of, 'Oh, let's get on, let's get on.' I'm thinking. Thinking where we go next.'

'We need to have a look through any possible sexual cases back in the day in Stornoway.'

'Yes, we do,' said Clarissa. 'That was a good line of attack. I think we'll pay a visit, but first,' she took out her phone, 'I'm going to talk to Als.'

Patterson looked over at her. 'Who would Als be?'

'Ross. I call him Als. Everybody else calls him Ross. Well, Hope sometimes calls him Alan, but you'll call him Ross because he's Ross. Okay? Everybody knows him as Ross. Don't call him Als because that's what I call him. He doesn't like it.'

'So why do you call him it?' asked Patterson.

'Because it's Als. He needs to be snappier. Needs a bit more joie de vivre about him. Do him good.'

'What are you going to call me?' asked Eric.

'I haven't decided that yet. Barely know you. At the moment, it's Mr Fidget.' Clarissa turned away and addressed the phone call to Ross.

'Als, I need you to do something for me. Beaton, Henderson and McNeil were all in Stornoway at the same time. The boss was there too. I need you to look at their times there and see if there were any sexual cases. Yes. I'll hold.'

Clarissa sat back in the little green car, staring up at the sky. 'Oh, I need to put the hood up because it looks like it is going to rain again.'

'What are you doing now? Can't we just get going?' said Patterson.

'No, we can't. What you can do is check the ferries and check the airport because we need to be over to Stornoway quick. See what gets us there faster.'

Clarissa sat waiting before hearing Ross back on the other end of the line.

'Quick run-through. I can't find any official records. Nothing. All the old stuff's been loaded up. There's nothing on the system.'

'Well, I think I'd better take a proper look. You know how some of this stuff never gets put down properly. If you see

Hope or Macleod, tell them I'm on my way to Stornoway and tell them I'll be calling him to find out what he knows. Time to make tracks, though. Thanks, Als.'

The rain started to fall, and Clarissa jumped out of the car to pull up the convertible hood. Once back inside, she started the engine and got a look from Patterson.

'What?'

'I haven't told you where we're going yet.'

'We're heading back towards Inverness because you're going to get a flight or we're going to go straight through to Ullapool. I hope you got a bag with you.' Patterson looked at her. 'A bag for the murder team. You always carry a bag. You don't want to wear the same pants for three days in a row.'

'Did you ever think, Sergeant, that it'd be better to have a proper car?'

Clarissa could feel the anger welling up inside her. 'What does a proper car look like?' she asked.

'Well, something with a roof for a start. Something that doesn't look like you're the new Colombo.'

Clarissa spun the wheel, hit the accelerator and spun the back end of the car around. She drove quickly to the end of the car park, spun the car again out onto the road, and tore away from the care home. Paterson looked somewhat dishevelled in his seat.

'Seatbelt! You need to buckle up for this ride,' said Clarissa. 'Get your head back into that phone of yours and tell me where we're going. You stick with me, Patterson. You may know all the procedures, you may have a name for yourself, but Urquhart will show you a bit of style.'

Chapter 14

Where is it? thought Hope McGrath. *Where is it?*

A van matching the description of one that was seen outside Ellie Fraser's house was discovered heading north through the Fife area of Scotland. Hope McGrath had put out instructions for a manhunt. Macleod had given her the authority to use whatever resources she could find. While it had taken time to get things going, they had narrowed down the area that the van was in to just south of the Cairngorms.

It was a long way away from where they'd started. Galashiels being in the south of Scotland and now the van was thought to be somewhere possibly north of Perth. Hope had jumped in the car and come down to meet with the sergeant coordinating the investigation in the area. She'd also grabbed her new start that Macleod had organised and was slightly shocked by what she'd found.

DC Susan Cunningham was well known to Hope. In fact, she was well known to most of the station. It wasn't ever because of her detective qualities or due to her police record, rather, it was her nighttime activities. She had long, blonde hair and a trim figure to die for and one that was certainly remarked upon. Not that it would've bothered Hope, but Susan had that flirty feel to her and she was always egging the guys on.

Even Hope, who was not afraid to look good, found her open flaunting a bit much, and she'd been surprised that Macleod had chosen her. Seoras certainly wouldn't have approved of that, but he must have had his reasons because the DCI always did. *More than that*, Hope thought, *she is wearing similar clothing to me. Boots, jeans, t-shirt, but not a leather jacket. That one is suede.*

When Hope had pulled up in the car outside the station that morning, she shouted for Cunningham to get inside. She had heard her turn to a couple of male officers entering the building. There were a few calls and a few choice words that Hope would rather not hear. On the drive down, she'd had to lay down the law of what she had expected. Cunningham hadn't taken it too well. The girl was twenty-three. Hope stopped herself. The girl. When did Hope get to any age when she started calling adults, girls?

On finding the sergeant responsible for coordinating the search, Hope stayed with Cunningham while he briefed them on what had happened. The van currently was last seen just north of Perth, heading off into the hills.

'Have we got the helicopter up?' asked Hope.

'Yes, it's up and on its way, but if they're hiding in the trees, they're going to be hard to spot.'

'What about feet on the ground? How many cars did you bring out here?'

'As many as I can spare. It's not that easy. You can't just whip everyone out.'

'No one's saying it is, Sergeant. I'm just asking,' said Hope.

'Here, this is the frequency we're working on through air-wave in the hills. It won't be that easy to get communications, especially if they go down into some of the valleys.'

'Nothing new there,' said Hope. 'Susan,' she said, turning to her fellow officer, 'I want you to make sure you keep giving our position. It's very easy to suddenly get out of contact and then people don't know where we are.'

'Are we not going to stay here?'

'No. We haven't got that many cars. We'll get out on the road as well. Sergeant, give me somewhere to search.'

Ten minutes later, Hope and Susan Cunningham were driving up into the Cairngorms. She saw the helicopter pass over the top of them and Hope kept the wheel, although normally Ross would drive her.

'You sure you wouldn't like me to drive?'

'I know my mind,' said Hope. 'Just keep focused on the maps. Where are we looking for next?'

'Take the left, left, and the right. We're following that road round. It's about five miles before you get to the next junction.'

It was raining, but the cloud wasn't too low, and Hope thought the Cairngorms, as ever, looked spectacular. Large sweeping mountains and then long lochs with rolling shades of green and brown. She loved it up here. Hope had come up here with John twice on holiday, but they were a nightmare to search over. She'd prefer an urban landscape. Here there was so much land off-road and they didn't have the manpower to sweep across that.

'All units, van spotted heading North, grid position...'

Hope watched her colleague taking down the grid position and then firing it into the map. 'About half a mile away,' said Susan. 'Turn the car around.'

Hope braked hard, then reversed the car in a quick three-point turn, racing back down the road.

'Up to the right!'

Hope followed the instruction, the car racing up to seventy miles an hour down what was a narrow road. Another car came around the corner and the gap between them was tight. Hope heard the trees brush against the wing mirror on the passenger side. To give Susan credit, she mentioned nothing about it.

An update came through on the radio and Susan plotted again where the helicopter had said the van was. Hope was directed left, off onto a forest path, and raced along it. She'd always fancied being a rally driver at some point. It always seemed such fun, but here, as the trees passed her by, she realised how terribly scary the whole thing was. One minor mistake and she'd slide off. Who knew if you could survive the impact, but this was the risk. So far, the killers had been perfect. They'd got away without leaving a trail behind, but this could be the one. This could break the case open. Hope kept the accelerator down hard.

'There,' shouted Susan.

Hope slammed on the brakes. Despite the wetness, some dust and pine cones flew up off to the left. Hope could see a van's side door open, and someone dressed in black running around it. Cunningham was out the door. Hope took off her seatbelt and followed her.

The ground around the trees before the opening where the van had reached was lumpy, and keeping a stride was difficult. Cunningham was up ahead, and Hope watched her race towards the van. As she got close, there was a sudden whoomph, and the van went up in flames. Someone had poured petrol and had ignited it, and Hope saw that person running in from the side.

Cunningham had been overcome by the sudden heat and knocked back towards the ground. The man, for it surely had to be a man at that size, ran over and grabbed Cunningham, wrapping an arm around her neck. He hauled her to her feet as he saw Hope coming into the clearing.

There were no weapons she could see, but he knew what he had, gun or otherwise. The man dragged Cunningham away, but Hope saw he was struggling with her and decided the best course was to go for the man. He wasn't watching her at first, dragging Cunningham by the neck, hauling her towards a gap in the trees that led out to somewhere open.

Hope put her head down and charged. Just as she was reaching them, she saw the knife produced from behind the man. He swung it in a long arc, causing Hope to rear up suddenly. As the arm went past, he came back again with the blade, but this time, Hope was able to block the arm with her own.

Undeterred, the man head butted Hope, causing her to fall to the ground. The man let go of Cunningham and swept down with the knife. Hope was dazed, but she was alert enough to roll over to one side. He turned and ran.

Hope got groggily up to her feet. 'Get after him,' she shouted, but Cunningham was wheezing on the ground. He had clearly throttled her badly. Hope hauled herself up on her feet, saw the man running through a gap in the trees.

'Call it in. Let's get him surrounded. There's nowhere for him to go,' said Hope.

Then she heard it, a whining buzz that got louder and louder. Hope could see a large grassy plain in front of her and running through the middle of it was a track. She watched in disbelief as coming towards her, and descending, was a small microlight. It touched down on the track, and the man in black kept running towards it. The microlight, once it landed, turned and faced the other direction.

Hope put her head down and ran for all she was worth, and she was gaining. She was quick, and she saw the man try to get into the pod at the front of the microlight. The engine was still going, and he was climbing in as they pulled away, realising she was close. The microlight raced forward, and Hope felt her lungs going. At any moment she felt she might overrun trip and fall, but she kept going hard as she could.

As the microlight lifted, she threw herself forward. A leg was still hanging out from the man in black climbing on board, and she grabbed hold of his boot. She was dragged along the ground, hanging onto it tightly as the microlight fought to get off the ground. She felt her backside bump several times over the rough ground, but she had her arm round the boot, in a deep hug, her head pinned close to the guy's leg.

He grabbed her hair, and he rained three punches down on the top of her head. Hope had no way of protecting herself. Her arms let go, and she slid along the road briefly before coming to a halt. As she turned over, she saw the microlight eventually lift into the air, disappearing out of sight.

'Are you all right?' It was Cunningham, behind her.

'Of course, I'm not bloody all right,' said Hope. 'Call it in. Microlight heading northeast. See if anybody else can track it.'

She hadn't even got the boot. She'd been hanging onto the boot. If she had got that off, then it would have been something. A size, maybe even DNA from inside, not that DNA so far had proved useful.

After Cunningham completed her call, she helped Hope up. Hope checked herself over. She was sore, and there'd be bruising, but everything seemed to move correctly. Yes, her head was ringing. You didn't get punched like that and not suffer for it, but again, they hadn't broken the skin. When they reached the car, Hope said that Cunningham should drive.

'Are you sure?'

'I've just been punched in the head several times. I'm not sure my focus is going to be correct. It's probably safer if you drive.'

As the car was turned around and headed back for the main road, Hope noted Cunningham kept staring at her. As they reached the main road, Hope put her hand up.

'I'm okay,' she said. 'Really, I'm okay. You don't need to keep looking at me.'

'I'm just impressed,' said Cunningham. 'Really, I'm impressed.' The woman went suddenly embarrassed, her cheeks becoming red.

'What is it?' asked Hope.

'It's you, isn't it?' said Cunningham. 'I kind of look up to you. A lot of us women do. You've made it under somebody like Macleod. Look at you, you look good, but you're also great at the job. I might look it, but I can't do what you can. That was quite something. What happened to me? I just got grabbed.'

Hope flung herself back in her seat, almost ready to laugh. 'Right, left, get up this road. If the microlight comes down, we want to be in the general area.'

Cunningham nodded and followed the directions. Hope looked over at her again. She'd been so put out by the woman's looks, and yet she thought Hope looked good. Hope laughed. When had she retreated into that worry about herself?

When she started with Macleod, she hadn't had that self-confidence. It always bugged her, the thing that always let her down, and here was Cunningham, seeing her as the example, a confident, can-do female detective. Her phone rang, and she picked it up, noting it was Macleod.

'Hope,' he said, 'you can stop looking for the kid. Stephen's been found.'

'Where?' said Hope.

'Inverness, my coffee house. The one I always go to. He was found in their toilet, bound and gagged, but otherwise unharmed.'

'I've just left the van.'

'Who was in it?'

'One. Just one person. Cornered him, but he jumped into a microlight in the middle of the Cairngorms. I had a hold on him, but well…'

'I doubt that Ellie Fraser is in the Cairngorms,' said Macleod. 'They've taken her somewhere else. We'll have to get a heck of a break to find her now.'

'Agreed. We're going to hunt down this microlight though, see if we can catch it. I'm not holding out a lot of hope. It's a heck of a lot of ground to cover and we haven't got that amount of manpower.'

She closed down the call and realised that she was really sore from what she'd just done.

'That was the boss, Cunningham.'

'The DCI?'

'Yes. They found Stephen, the kid, in Inverness. He's unharmed. No sign of Ellie.' Hope hit the dashboard with her hand. 'Damn it. Bastard,' she said. She saw another call coming through. It was John, her partner. It wasn't a good time. Not now. She answered it anyway. 'John, it's not a good time. I can't…'

'Shush,' he said. 'Hope, you need to get here to the car hire place, to my work.'

'Why? What's the matter?' she asked, hearing the desperation in his voice. 'We've just found a body in the boot of a car returned to us. It's got no clothes on. It's a woman with no clothes on, but it's, it's…'

'What, John? What is it?'

'It's covered in whip marks, everywhere, whip marks, large welts. Hope, it's gross.'

'Have you called anyone?'

'Called the ambulance. They said they were calling the police. I thought you should know. I mean, you'll know what to do with this, won't you?'

'Yes,' said Hope. 'Just stay calm. I'm south of the Cairngorms. Somebody will be with you shortly. I'll see you soon. Try not to think about it.'

'What was that?' asked Cunningham.

'I think we're too late for Ellie,' said Hope. She picked up her phone again to call Macleod back.

Chapter 15

Hope had been driven back up to the station by Cunningham. She decided that her best bet was to debrief Stephen rather than visit the car firm of her partner where the body had been found. John would have to understand that they were up against time. Anything they could find out from Stephen may be more helpful to them than her going to make things smoother at his work.

She sent Cunningham on instead, telling her what to say to John, and that she'd have to take him through what would happen from then on. She also said that she should see if he needed counselling or help. *But John would be okay*, she believed. *He'd been through things before, including an attack in the hospital with her.*

She entered the police station and saw Macleod coming down the stairs. 'Where are you going?' she asked.

'You're in with the kid,' he said. 'I'm going to go up and see the body.'

'Cunningham's got it.'

'It's her first day, and she's a DC and it could get serious out there, press trying to ask questions.'

'But she can handle it, can't she? I mean, you picked her. You didn't pick a dummy.'

'A dummy,' said Macleod. 'No, I don't pick dummies. I don't have dummies around me. I've picked her because she's got a lot of qualities a certain other person used to have. Susan's also got similar weaknesses to what they had. She's not the same as you, Hope, but she's similar, and that's why I want her with you. Susan needs to learn from you how to get past those doubts, those fears. She needs to understand she's not just a good-looking person, she is a clever soul, and she can do a lot better for herself. But she won't learn that from me. She'll learn it from you.'

Hope stared down at him. 'She's not six foot with red hair though,' she laughed.

'No, she's not, but she likes you a lot. She looks up to you. They don't look up to old farts like me. When you took on the DI role, you're the one in charge, you're the boss up there. You're the boss in this section of the case. You've decided to go in and talk to the kid. It's the right decision. It's where we'll find most out, but I've got to make sure that everybody else is covered off. I've got to support, which is what I said I'd always do. You get me some information. I'll make sure Cunningham's all right and make sure everything's tidied up there. I've also got to field a phone call from Clarissa later on, so don't you think I'm getting it easy.'

'Phone call from Clarissa? Why? What's she on to?'

'There's been another card found. Apparently, each time there's been a card. The second one went to a care home to a DCI Anthony Henderson, but the care home put it in the bin. They thought it was a prank. Instead, it was a 3D card with a frieze on it and some poor guy getting his genitals cut off. Henderson used to be at Stornoway. Angus McNeil was

131

at Stornoway. Eileen Beaton was at Stornoway as well. Back when I wasn't so good. I'm afraid I wasn't very nice to Eileen in the past. You may remember I wasn't always so good with women.'

'Who says you're good with them now?' said Hope.

'You know what I mean,' said Macleod.

'Yes, I do,' she said, 'but I knew there was somebody good in there.'

A uniformed constable came down the stairs and the two of them stepped aside in a rather awkward moment as the man walked through. 'Inspector,' said the man to Macleod. 'Hope.' As the man turned away further down the stairs, Macleod looked back over at Hope. 'And that is why you'll be the future. I still get "Inspector."'

'Well, I can't change the grumpiness. It's how you get the best out of them anyway,' said Hope. 'I'm not you.'

'No, and many people are thankful for it,' he said. 'Right, I'm out of here. Go get me something.'

She turned and watched him descend the stairs. She'd always had the nagging doubt in her, was she good enough? Was she clever enough like he was? Once he'd got to know her, once he'd worked with her a few times, he'd had no doubt. Many a time she'd taken that and used that as her own confidence, but now she saw Cunningham look up to her.

Hope skipped up the stairs, heading to the interview room. Stephen was still shaking when Hope entered. There was a can of coke in front of him, a parent beside him, who seemed to be more in tears than Stephen was, as well as a specialist officer and Hope. Hope sat back, letting Kay, the specialist officer, speak first and run through the basic questions.

'How did you end up in the van, Stephen?' asked Kay.

'They were taking her, and I just wanted to help. She's good. Ellie's a friend. Then I got worried, and I hid in the van, and they got in. But they didn't see me, and then they got out, and they threw Ellie in and I lifted her mask.'

'When did they find you in it?'

'They drove so far, and then they opened it, and they saw me there. The man, he said, well, I don't speak language like that in front of mum.'

'Okay, did you know where you were?' asked Kay.

'No, it wasn't anywhere local, anywhere that I live, but it was a forest. There was a forest there and a car park, but there were no other cars. It was nighttime.'

'Stephen,' said Hope, 'do you remember what the voices sounded like?'

'Scottish, they all sounded Scottish,' he said, 'but different Scottish. One was from near us. I could hear the sound. It was closer to Glasgow. Others were different Scottish.'

'Okay, so we'll get you to listen to some voices later and see if you can pick up some areas where they're from. Were they all men or were there women?'

'At least one was a woman. I think the others were men, but not all the same. One had a really deep voice.'

'How did you feel when they opened the door on you?'

'Scared,' he said, 'but they took me by the hand. They weren't nasty to me, not until they tied me up. Instead, they took me into the woods.'

'And they did what?' asked Hope. She was nervous, fearing for the boy.

'They gave me crisps,' he said, 'and I sat with two of them. Then they put me in a car, and we drove to a house. I didn't see Pastor Ellie after that. She went off in the van again with two of them.'

'What did they do with you at the house?'

'They put me in a room. They covered my eyes and put me into a room, so I never saw the outside of the house.'

'What was your room like?'

'There was a bed,' he said, 'to sleep in. There was a TV, and they put the TV on. Although I wasn't allowed to watch the news, I could watch kids' programs. I'm fourteen, but they only let me watch kids' programs. Some of them were too young. And they brought me food and drink and just told me to stay quiet.'

'Did you?' asked Hope.

'Yes. They weren't bad to me. I was scared, but they weren't bad. I said to them, "When can I go home?" They told me soon. They told me it would only be a day or so.'

'What did they do after that?'

'They put me in the car, blindfolded me until we'd left the house. Then once on the road, they'd let me look out, told me to keep quiet and not to make a fuss. I didn't. We drove somewhere, and then they went round the back of some shops. That was when they tied me up. They took me into the rear of a shop and into the toilets and tied me up and left me in there. Said that somebody would come soon, and people did.'

'Did you see their faces at all?' asked Hope.

'Never, they wore these masks,' said the boy. He had a haunted look about him though and Kay, the specialist officer, tapped Hope on the shoulder, indicating she would take it from here.

'Is there something you're not telling us, Stephen? It's okay to tell us. If you need help, we can help you. It's okay.'

'I heard screaming when I was in my room from somewhere

in the house,' he said. 'It was scary. I think it was a woman screaming. It might have been…' Tears were coming down from his eyes. 'I think it might have been Pastor Ellie. There were loud cracks all the time.'

'Cracks,' said Kay, 'How so?'

'Cracking and then weeping and yelling and more cracking, like a snap,' he said.

Hope could tell what it was. They whipped her in the same building he was in. *Dear God*, she thought, *if that kid finds out one day*.

'Did you see anything outside of your room?' Kay asked him.

'I opened the curtains once, just slightly so nobody could see, and it was daytime.' He said, 'There was a sign, but it wasn't where I was. It was in a house close to it, not far away. We weren't on a housing estate, we were out in the country and this other house was beyond us. I had to look through the trees and I could just about make out some letters. It had something, and then W-E-R. I think there was a space and then H-O, and I couldn't see the rest. I tried, but I couldn't. Underneath there was a I-N-A-B, or it might have been an L-N-A-B, I don't know.'

The boy's mother had sat the whole time holding one of his hands, and Hope could see the tears welling up in her. They ran through the story a second time trying to clarify elements, but there wasn't much to say. Clearly, the killers had no intention of killing the kid. In fact, they treated him well, handing him back in as safe a fashion as they could without revealing themselves.

These aren't psychopathic people, thought Hope. These *are people with a cause*. When she exited the room, she walked back to her office, picked up the phone and called Macleod.

135

'How's it going up there?'

'John's fine,' said Macleod, and Hope breathed an enormous sigh of relief. She thought he would be, but you could never be sure. After all, the previous body had knocked Clarissa for six.

'The car was hired under a false name, and it's also only gone about thirty miles before being brought back. Hope, they know you and they know me. Whoever's doing this has done a lot of research, but I don't understand why we're being targeted. Maybe Clarissa can find that out in Stornoway, but you weren't there.'

'We have had a couple of cases back there.'

'But none of them link into this,' said Macleod. 'I don't get it at the moment. How's the kid?'

'He'll be all right. He's unharmed. They were good to him, fed him, looked after him, kept him away from what they did to Ellie, except he heard it. Clearly, they couldn't keep him too far away.'

'That bothers me,' said Macleod. 'They don't see him as collateral. There's a chief focus here from these people. They're doing it for a specific reason, and they think they're right in doing it. There's a moral thing going on. I wonder if they're challenging us as the police. They see us as having failed them.'

'Maybe,' said Hope, 'but Stephen said something. He'd looked out the window, and he saw another house close by. We got some letters for a sign by the house, but they don't seem to make sense, W-E-R, space, H-O. The other is, space, L-N-A-B. What is LNAB?'

'Get it to Ross,' said Macleod. 'When you get stuff like this, don't think about it. Get it to Ross. It's not about people, it's a straight-word scramble. You need to work out what words can go around it. This has got Ross written all over it. Just give it to him and trust him.'

'I will do, sure. How is Cunningham holding up?'

'A little raw, but she's doing all right, but I had to give her a brief lesson about the press.'

'Why? What do they want?'

'What do you mean "what do they want"? The old farts here, so they don't want to talk to me because they know they'll get a mouthful. Oh, here's the new young detective constable. It's the same thing all over again. They wanted her up to talk to them next. You've got to teach her how to own that, Hope. On your terms, not theirs, teach her what's important. She'll listen to you.'

'How do you know she's going to listen to me? Just because she thinks I'm the bee's knees now. She'll find out what I'm like.'

'Because you found out what I'm like, and you listened to me,' he said. 'Both of them I've brought in, they'll be good. Patterson's got to loosen up. He's too stiff. That's why I've put him with Clarissa. She'll break it in him, but he's solid, understands the job, understands how to detect. He'll be good. Cunningham will be a leader one day. She'll rally people around her like you do. She'll deal with them civilly, but in a way to get the best out of them like you do. That's why she's with you, because you and I won't be around forever. Hopefully, you'll be around a lot longer than me.'

'Right, I better get this to Ross because they're not hanging about, are they?'

'No,' said Macleod.

Hope closed the call. He was worried. After all these years, she could tell when he was worried. Maybe Ross could find him something. Either that or Jona was going to have to come up with it.

She walked back down the stairs and suddenly felt a rather sore point just at the top of her thigh towards her buttock. It was where she'd scraped along the ground, bouncing up and down. She touched it and felt the pain.

Bruise on bruise, she thought. *Always takes it out of you, this thing.* She reached up and touched the scar across her cheek where she'd been hit by the acid when she'd saved Macleod's partner, Jane. She thought about what she'd done.

Macleod had once called it beautiful and said that every time he saw the scar, he thought of what Hope had done for him. She smiled and hoped that the old dog wasn't going anywhere soon.

Chapter 16

James Clark spun and let his feet roll out of bed before slowly clambering up onto them. Lifting the dressing gown off the back of the door, he wrapped it around himself, and then searched briefly for his slippers. He had been woken by the clatter of the letter box and would pick up the morning mail before making breakfast. He took the stairs slowly, one at a time, first one foot on, then the other, holding onto the handrail the whole time.

He'd resisted going to a home, knowing he was okay to live on his own. Surely Dornoch wasn't a rough place to live. It was also by the coast, and he enjoyed nothing more than taking a stroll, albeit not a quick one, and then sitting on a bench to watch the sea. Days seem to pass quickly now, filled with getting up and feeding yourself. The mundane processes of life, such as washing, cleaning the dishes, and occasionally going outside to enjoy the fresh air.

He'd received a rather puzzling call several days before from Eileen Newton, someone he'd worked with only briefly. James Clark had never got above constable, but then that's all he wanted to do. You did your time. Clocked off. Went home. He'd never wanted a promotion, but he never really wanted

139

much.

As he reached the bottom of the stairs, he opened the door to the front room of his two-up, two-down house. A large board filled the room, but all the trains were stationary. This had been what he'd loved, nothing more than sitting down and watching them go round and round. The collection in here was beyond price. Sure, they could take it and put it back in the original boxes and sell it. It would be worth a small fortune, but nothing compared to the time he'd spent letting the trains pass by. Nothing compared to the effort spent in building the surrounding models: the landscape, the bridges, the station with all the people, each one with a story to tell.

James hadn't enjoyed being a police officer. People were so complicated, but here in his world of trains, he was happy. Not that this was as big as what they had been. Before he'd had to retire and move up to Dornoch, he'd had an enormous set that went through three rooms of the house. It nearly broken his heart when he'd had to sell some of it.

He closed the door, turned, and shuffled over towards the front door and saw the letters lying on the carpet. He picked them up. There were at least five, but he didn't look at them, and instead shuffled back through to the kitchen, placing the letters on the kitchen table. He took out two slices of bread, popped them in the toaster, and then put the kettle on to boil.

Coffee and toast, two slices every day for the last twenty-five years. Real butter, of course, nothing else. When the toaster popped, he took the slices, buttered them, poured himself instant coffee, and sat down at the table, ready to sort out breakfast. He wouldn't touch the letters until he'd finished eating, and it took him ten minutes as he thoughtfully chewed through.

His mind was on a Hornby diesel train he'd seen and working out if he could actually afford it. He could, of course, but he liked to ponder purchases. After all, they were significant.

Having finished the toast, he looked at the letters in front of him. Well, that one was the electricity bill. The next one, some flyer. The one after that the subscription to *Model Trains* magazine that was due about now. No surprise in opening that one, but then there was a plain brown envelope.

He glowered at it, slightly disturbed, remembering that Eileen had told him about a plain brown envelope that had come to her. Slowly, he cut it open and pulled out a card from inside. He looked at the front, almost slightly bemused.

There was a man squatting, an unusual position to be in, but what bemused him was that the man was squatting on somebody else's arm. At least the arm was… well, he couldn't be sure. Was the arm? No, people didn't sit like that. Why would you be wanting to put your arm up there, your hand up to clean someone's bottom?

It was all very bemusing to him, but the envelope was brown, and the card was like Eileen's in that there was nothing inside, just this picture on the front.

James Clark stood up and walked over to a dresser on the far side of the kitchen. He pulled open a drawer and looked inside for an address book. He flicked through and eventually came upon a number; Seoras Macleod. He was sure he'd seen him on the telly a few days ago asking about this. Maybe it wasn't important what the card said, maybe it was, but the right thing to do was to call it in. Macleod would know what to do after all. He was one of those higher-up ones paid to do it. James Clark had always been a constable, and therefore, it was his duty to give it to the person who would decide.

141

* * *

They had caught the last ferry over and found some accommodation for the night. Clarissa was shattered, but she was also struggling. She hadn't cleared the image of Derek Clark from her mind. When she closed her eyes, she could see it again.

She'd done the right thing. She'd gone to see if he was alive, gone to help in whatever way she could. But what she had seen was chilling her to the core. Four times in the night she'd woken up, and during one of them, she'd taken out her mobile and called Frank.

The poor man didn't know what to do. He looked after greens and fairways, not traumatised detective sergeants, but he'd stayed on. Had said he would be there all night. Told her to ring again if she woke up.

She was finding herself drawn closer and closer to him, albeit not in the way she'd thought. Clarissa had imagined going to art galleries. She'd dreamt of strolls along the beach, or even the odd picnic, nice candlelit dinners. Not torrid outbursts where she couldn't tell him anything.

Well, she'd find out if he was truly invested or not. He'd either think of her as a nutter, or worse.

Eric Patterson had slept well that night as he told Clarissa at breakfast. This wasn't helping. He then said that they should pop along, introduce themselves formally, and see if they could find time with those who were there at the station. Maybe get them all together to inform them about what they were looking for and to see if anyone could help.

Clarissa had sat looking at a couple of fried eggs as he'd gone on about what plans they should make.

'People don't talk about things when everyone's there. You

get them on the quiet. The important thing here is not to have everything documented. It's to understand the case. If there's something in the past that hasn't been documented, it's likely that it wasn't done so because it wasn't good. It wasn't something easily explained, or at worst, it was covering up for someone. What we don't want to do is to say, "Here, all your faults can be brought out into the light. Just talk to DC Patterson."'

Patterson had almost snarled at her, which she considered good because it was the first decent reaction she had got out of him. The man needed to toughen up a bit, show a bit of spunk. They used that word still, didn't they?

At half-past eight, Clarissa and Eric entered Stornoway Police Station and spoke to the desk sergeant. An older detective came down, shook her hand, and took her inside to his office.

'I'm not looking to shake things up,' said Clarissa, 'but there's a possible link between several people who worked here, Beaton, McNeil, Macleod, and Henderson. Is there anything from around that time that would be…well…maybe a bit suspicious, swept under the carpet the way things used to be done?'

'This is off the record, isn't it?' asked the detective.

'Of course. We're trying to track down a killer, but the killer is pointing out something about here. I need to work out what it is.'

'You need to talk to Donny Nails. Macleod won't know who Donny Nails is. He lives up north, near Ness. I'll give him a phone call, say you're coming. He's a bit deaf at the moment, but he knew everything back then.'

'Donny Nails? Bit of a tough nut, is he?' asked Clarissa.

143

'No, he just..., he wouldn't trim his nails properly. Donny always rather liked them. He would stare at them and point and go, 'Look at them, how well I've done with them today.' He was quite effeminate, which back in those days, of course, got you a name. Not that he was that way inclined, but he liked to look good. Snappy hair, snappy dress, and nails manicured, and he wasn't too keen on getting his hands dirty.'

Clarissa laughed. 'Give me the address. We'll pop up that way and stay out of here for the minute.'

The drive up to Ness was an enjoyable one, as the rain had ceased the day before. Clarissa liked the wind through her hair, but clearly, it was disturbing Eric Patterson's neat combing from the morning. As soon as she parked the car up, he had a comb out, making himself look presentable again.

'You're going to have no hair left,' said Clarissa, 'the time you spend with that.'

'If you would just drive with the top up, it wouldn't be necessary to keep trying to maintain an appearance.'

'You're a police officer, so maybe you'll understand this guy.'

Eric looked at her with daggers as Clarissa marched up to the front door of the house. It was out on its own on a separate croft and looked rather dilapidated. Clarissa wondered if anybody actually lived in there and saw the slightly stained net curtains. She banged on the door to find it being opened by a man in a large tank top. He was about five foot four, and she finally found someone she could look down at.

'You that Urquhart woman?'

'That's me,' said Clarissa. 'This is that Patterson man. Can we come in?'

'Suppose so. Come.'

They marched through into a front room with a carpet that

had seen much better days. Clarissa could count the cigarette burns on it and the dirty marks, but she said nothing as she plunked herself down in a wooden seat. There was no sofa, and she wondered, *Is this the pristine man of long ago?*

'There's a pleasant fire on. Keeps the water going. Hope you don't mind.'

'No,' said Clarissa. 'I actually wanted to come and talk to you about the force here a long time ago, back in the days of Macleod and…'

'Beaton. Yes, I know, Angus McNeil. That's a long time ago. McNeil never shut up about my fingers. Dirty man, so he was.'

'In what way?' asked Patterson.

'He didn't keep his hands clean. Didn't wash properly. I washed properly, and I was the butt of his jokes. They wouldn't stand for it nowadays.'

'That's true,' said Clarissa. 'But do you have any information? Was there anybody in any cases you were looking at that who you thought might be a sexual predator of some sort?'

'There was a reverend, Donald Anderson, out on the west side. There were lots of rumours about him, but they were quashed. Your Macleod, he was just a new start. Very early days with him, but Anderson had these rumours around him about certain boys being interfered with, but like I said, everything was quashed.'

'You wouldn't know the names of the boys, would you?'

'Well, a couple of them were MacIver, and a couple of them were Macleod.'

Clarissa raised her eyes, and Patterson looked at her. 'If you're going to narrow down names up here on this island,' said Clarissa, 'the last two won't cut it. It's a stampede in the co-op whenever you announced those names over the Tannoy.

145

You can do better than that,' said Clarissa to the man. 'You were an officer. We don't forget stuff like that.'

The man laughed at her. 'Oh, I know you, Urquhart.' He turned and grinned at her. 'Why did you go to the art side?'

'Because I was interested in it. I know about it. Why do you ask?'

'Because we always thought you'd be good working serious crime.'

'Oh, it is serious crime,' said Clarissa.

'It's just pictures and money,' said the man. 'Well, I'll get you your names. You won't have to shake me down.'

He marched over to a dresser, pulled out a pencil, and started writing names down. Clarissa gave a grin. *Bloody Philistine*, she thought, but she knew what he meant. Sometimes the art crime was ridiculed. Who cared if you lost that stuff? The insurance company, that's who cared, but some people cared enough to kill for it.

Donny Nails turned around and marched over to Clarissa, handing her the list. 'About five or six there. They're all grown men now, of course. I don't have the addresses. You might need the addresses, but you know what this place is like. If you can ask the right person, they'll know everything. There's no private business up here, but I guess you'll know that Urquhart, won't you?' He laughed. 'Blimey, Clarissa Urquhart in my house.'

When they left the building, Patterson looked a little be-mused. 'He obviously seemed to know you.'

'Lot of people in the force know me,' said Clarissa.

'Why is that?'

'I punched an Assistant Chief Constable once. It was back in the day.'

'What did he do?'

'He said, "Tell that bitch to get in line."'

'Did you get busted for it, or did they do him?'

'That was back in the day. Oh, I got a reprimand, but he got a bloody nose and he got laughed at for most of the rest of his career. Served him right. He was a crap officer.'

Clarissa could feel the stares of Patterson as she drove back from Ness. They would have some phone work to do, look up some public records, track down who these people were. If they started over on the west side with Donald Anderson's former church and expand out from there, maybe they could find them. It was time for Patterson to learn the old cliche, that you had to dig until something came up, but some stuff wasn't on the end of your computer.

Chapter 17

Macleod walked back into the office tired after working at the latest crime scene. His new secretary brought him through a coffee, for which he was very grateful, and he sat behind the desk dwelling on it for a moment. He placed a call down to Hope, asking that she pull in the team, including Clarissa, via webcam if necessary.

Although he had set up two sides to the investigation, he wanted to keep them linked and make sure that they worked with each other. He was also keen to see how his new DCs were getting on. It wasn't unusual for others to come in and help the team, but he was looking at these two as possible permanent additions.

He was barely thirty seconds into thinking about this when his telephone rang, and the secretary said the press were looking for comment. Without even thinking, he said, 'Tell them that the time for comment will come and at that point, there'll be a press conference. Currently, there's no further comment.'

It was a hard game to play with the press because sometimes you wanted them. You needed information put out into the mass media. Sometimes people responded. But right now he knew what they would be doing - trying to stir up an anti-church platform. Either that or those on the other side would stir it up as common decency gone out the window.

Neither was appropriate. He was convinced that in the past somebody had been hurt, but by who and how? He wasn't sure. Clearly, there was abuse involved, probably sexual. That you would kill somebody by using sex toys was bizarre and abhorrent, but he tried to understand why they would do it. He wasn't convinced they were thrill seekers, but rather, it might have been the other way around.

Where are the original victims, though, and the original perpetrators of the crime? Were the current victims the ones that caused the abuse or was it just simply an attack on the religious environment? Macleod wasn't sure and did not know why it was spreading across different denominations. If the original crimes had been done in a care home or orphanage, it would be under the umbrella of one denomination. These ministers and pastors were being pulled out of the woodwork here, there, and wherever.

He needed to think because that's where cases got solved, but he also needed more information. That's why he had kept Ross here. Ross was an exemplary officer out in the field, but they needed to search into a lot of history and Ross was the coordinator for that. Let Clarissa kick up a hornet's nest. Find out what people don't want to say. Let Hope go through the procedures. Dig and find out who had done what to whom. They all had their abilities, and he had to let them get on with it.

There came a knock at the door. 'Enter,' said Macleod.

'Seoras, we're ready for you.'

'Thank you,' he said. He looked down at this cup of coffee.

He'd barely got through the first quarter of it. He grabbed the cup and walked down the stairs into the main office. There was a sudden hush falling, and he saw them look up as he entered. He placed his mug down on the table, stood, and looked at them all. Macleod was good at reading people, and he could tell this room was a fearful one.

'We'll get them,' he said. 'We will get them. It's just a matter of how quickly we get them, but have no doubt, we will pull these people to justice. First, though, is Clarissa on?'

'I'm on the screen,' said a voice suddenly. Macleod looked to his right and saw the giant conference screen that had been wheeled into the office. There, on a webcam in a hotel room, was Clarissa with the new DC, Patterson, pacing behind her.

'Update, please,' said Macleod.

'We've got a possible incident,' said Clarissa. 'I won't be able to get to everyone today, but we will by tomorrow. A certain minister, Donald Anderson, has been flagged up.'

'West side?' asked Macleod.

'That one.'

'I remember him. It was my early days,' said Macleod. 'Had little to do with it, though. McNeil took it. If you need anything further, go down to Leverburgh and talk to him. He's a grumpy git, but he's still intact up top,' said Macleod.

'Oh, I've dealt with those sorts of people before,' said Clarissa. Before Macleod could say anything, she continued. 'There are rumours that he may have interfered with boys. I'm not sure how true that is. I'm also worried that he could be next if he's at the centre of this. Unfortunately, I can't find him now. I'll do more kicking tomorrow. See what I can come up with.'

'Good,' said Macleod. 'Make sure we cover that off and find him. I don't need another body. How are you getting on,

Patterson?' asked Macleod and then corrected himself. 'Sorry, Eric, how are you getting on?'

'Fine.'

Well, that wasn't convincing, thought Macleod. *Still, takes time to build up a good relationship.* 'Don't forget to use Eric if you need a little more of a formal approach,' Macleod said to Clarissa, who raised her eyebrows.

'I can be as formal as the next person.' Macleod heard the word 'rottweiler'. It was quiet, very quiet, but he scanned the room with his eyebrows raised just to make sure everyone knew he had heard it.

'Jona,' he said, noticing the Asian woman at the back. 'Anything come through from the cards?'

'Clean as a whistle. You can buy the envelopes anywhere. The postmarks are from all over the country. These people are not messing about. They're covering off the bases, Seoras.'

'Well, that's a pity,' he said. 'Hope, where are you at?'

'They are covering off their bases. I went to speak to Steven, the abducted boy, today. We've got a link to where he was being held. Ross is working through that now. Outside of that, they treated him well. He clearly wasn't meant to be the victim and he shouldn't have been there, but they didn't despatch him. They didn't simply throw him out of the van. They actually took care of him. Despite tying him up and dropping him at your coffee house, he was unharmed.'

'I'm checking through the CCTV as well, but the trouble was they blindfolded Steven before he got there. He's not even sure what car he was in and the alley at the rear hasn't got CCTV. The CCTV on the street front has got cars galore, passing by. These people aren't stupid,' said Ross. 'Somebody amongst them has got a clever head.'

'And it is these people,' said Macleod. 'That means somebody will slip. Somebody will drop one at some point, and they have. We need to get that address sorted, Ross. That's your top priority.'

'Understood, sir. While I'm on my feet, I have some information about our victims.'

'Really?'

'Just made the connection, sir. Discovered it just before you came down. I haven't had time to explore it any further. Hugh Barkley, Derek Clark, and Ellie Fraser were all together at University.'

'Studying divinity?'

'No, sir. All together in Edinburgh before their divinity degrees, studying various other courses. I haven't been able to get much else. Still checking through which courses. I don't know if they knew each other, but it's certainly a possible connection.'

'Good work, Ross,' said Macleod. 'It's more than a possible connection.'

'Seoras,' said Hope from the side, 'Can I suggest that Ross and Cunningham make their way down to Edinburgh? Chase up that connection.'

'No,' said Macleod. 'I've got the helm here. You go. This could be the big one. There's nothing else you're going to pull out of the bag with the bodies. Jona's got the mark on that. When it comes through, I'll tell you what it is. You chase this lead. Clarissa's got her end. You've got yours. Ross stays here. I just said his priority is getting that address, and we'll need somebody to go to that if it comes through. Besides, Cunningham went to university, didn't you?'

'Yes, sir.'

'Yes, Seoras. Look, everybody on this team, you need to understand, I'm the same as any other officer. We go by first names, okay? So, it's Seoras. Everybody got that?'

There was a general mummer, and then Ross put his hand up. 'I think people are just a little afraid of you, sir.'

Macleod tucked his head to one side and looked at Ross. 'You don't help with that constant platitude.' He knew it was too strong just as soon as he said it. 'But it is appreciated, Ross,' he continued.

'Right. I've been thinking through this, and the other thing we need to do is find where this lot are purchasing the devices from. Our first one was choked to death on a sexual aid. We've just had a person who's been whipped, and they have all been interfered with. It's not pretty to think about, but these things can be bought. Jona, if you tie up with Ross about the sizes and shapes, maybe Ross you can get into the shops. Get a few of these constables to open up their eyes, find out about the other side of life.

'If we can find where they've been purchasing, we might get CCTV. A lot of those shops carry it because they don't know what sort of customer they're going to get. I don't care if it's seedy or not, they've got to understand that we're not after them and they need to help us because this will not help them. Stories like this break and they'll be getting accused of generating such a culture. We go in polite, but we go in with the firm message that we're here to help them by helping us, not to bring them into it. Okay.'

'You can also get this stuff online, sir,' said Ross. Several people flipped their head round at him. 'Not that I've done that personally,' he said. There was a slight snigger.

'Just to let you know, sir, sorry, Seoras,' said a young

constable, 'I was approached today by the press and offered money.'

'Ross, get the details. Get one sergeant downstairs to deal with it. I assume we didn't take any money,' said Macleod.

'Of course not, sir. Sorry, Seoras.'

'Good. You can expect this. This is going national. The key thing is if somebody approaches you, no comment, report it. Do not engage at all. Sounds like you've done right. We feed tit-bits out and the case gets derailed. More than that, the people who are doing this can get a jump on us. Nothing leaves these rooms. I'll not insult you by saying, do you know that? But just in case anybody doesn't, you'll have the full weight of Clarissa on you.'

'Not yourself?' asked the constable.

'I deal with the serious stuff. Don't think she won't sort you out. Right, heads down, everyone. Clarissa, Eric, get some sleep, get up early, get over to the west side. Get me an answer of what went on there and if it's involved. Hope, you and Cunningham, get down to Edinburgh. Take the night, head off first thing in the morning.'

'We go now,' said Hope, looking over at Cunningham. Macleod could see the sudden despair on Cunningham's face. She looked tired.

'Okay. Ross, we're here until whenever, as per usual. Find where they held the kid. If you need any help with that address, come and see me upstairs.'

'I'll have it for you,' he said, and Macleod went to turn away but then turned back suddenly. He lifted his coffee cup and drained it and then put it back down.

'Pull together,' he said. 'We're off here, there, and wherever, but pull together. That's how we get it done.' He turned and walked out the door, and a sudden bustle returned to the room. Macleod, however, didn't go upstairs. Instead, he walked down to the rear entrance to the building and stood waiting until he saw Hope pass by.

'I think you should drive,' he said.

She turned and saw him in the shadows. 'You what?'

'I think you should drive. Let her get a couple of hours of sleep on the way down.'

'She's younger than me,' said Hope.

'Susan's not used to the chase. She's not used to this. She's half-knackered in there. You said you were going down, and she nearly collapsed at the idea. We haven't even got going into the depths of it. She'll be good one day, Cunningham, but you're going to have to give her a hand for a while.'

'Okay,' said Hope. 'Okay. I'll play it your way.'

'No,' said Macleod. 'With her, you play it your way. I'm just saying because I don't think you caught it. She's tired.'

Hope gave a nod and then went to turn.

'They're bad these,' said Macleod. 'When I said they whipped her, they did more than that. We're thinking she was alive and was whipped to death. Whoever this is, they're not messing about. There's something deep here.' Hope stared at Macleod for a moment and then gave a nod.

'Pull together,' she said. 'You don't normally have to tell us to pull together.'

'We don't have a lot of new people normally. Go on, I'll give John a call for you tonight and make sure he's okay.'

'You don't have to do that. He's well.'

'I'm the one stuck at base. I'm the one that'll have time. Go find out what that's all about.'

He watched Hope leave and then Cunningham came running

down the stairs behind her, a small bag over her shoulder. As she went to open the door, he called out.

'Susan,' said Macleod. She paused and looked over, but then almost respectively bowed her head.

'Don't do that,' he said. 'It's just me. How's it going so far?'

'It's okay, but I don't think I should really discuss it in front of you without Hope being present. She's my boss or, rather, Clarissa is my boss.'

'Good, I hate it when people don't tell me I've said something wrong, but there's something you need to know. Don't fake it in front of her. If you're tired, just tell her. Be honest with Hope. I know you want to impress her. I know she's someone you've looked up to and you should, but you're not her yet. You'll get there, but just take your time in doing so, okay?'

'Yes, Seoras,' she said. She went to open the door, but she turned back. 'Thanks.'

A cry of 'hurry up' came from outside and Susan threw the bag over her shoulder again and ran outside for the car. Macleod watched the two women drive off into the night, heading for Edinburgh.

You picked that one right, he thought. *Clarissa wouldn't get her. She's never really got Hope.*

Chapter 18

Clarissa watched her colleague, Eric Patterson, approaching the man clad in a boiler suit standing beside a large cow. Patterson looked out of place, tailored jacket and crisp shoes suited the more urban setting of Glasgow or Edinburgh. Out here on the west side of Lewis, he looked strangely amiss.

The crofter before him was Angus Burns, a church elder from the time of Donald Anderson, and one on the list of people that Clarissa had drawn up. She'd spoken to several others that day, but achieved nothing to move the investigation forward. They were around at the time, but they knew nothing and all she'd had done was field Patterson's questions about her savage nature.

Constantly, he told her she was jumping in too hard, although he put it politely. After all, she was the sergeant. Eventually, Clarissa had got fed up with him, turned around, and told him he could do the next bloody interview.

She didn't understand why the guy was pushing. And now when she was struggling. After seeing that image, she hadn't slept at night. The corpse she'd found, mutilated in its bottom half, kept coming back to her. She'd rang Frank several times now, and in fairness to him, he never complained once. But she hadn't told Patterson.

The man was pernickety too; make a note of this, do this, do that. Clarissa didn't need to be told how to do the job after being in it for so long. There were rules and regulations, sure, but you learned how to approach people. Patterson said he didn't trust her not to butt in if he took the lead, so Clarissa, full of anger, told him, 'Fine, you can interview Angus Burns.'

She sat in the car watching. The conversation looked incredibly polite, but she couldn't lip-read them, so she was in the dark about what was going on. After ten minutes, Patterson returned to the car, sat down beside Clarissa, and gave a sigh.

'Well, what have you dug up?'

'The man knows nothing. He was an elder around the time, but he said the allegations were quite bizarre. Nobody really believed them. He said it was the ruin of a good minister.'

'Did he, now? Did you ask him about whether the elders quashed it, this allegation?'

'He said they found it very hard to.'

'Why?'

'He said it was because the woman that brought it forward and some of the other mothers were quite dominant in the community.'

'So, what now?' asked Clarissa.

Patterson looked at the piece of paper with names in front of him. 'I think we go back into town, see if we can dig up any more names. Maybe scroll through the records.'

'Whatever,' said Clarissa. She was meant to oversee the investigation, but now she just felt lopsided. *Why the hell was Als not with her? Als was good. She got on with Als, albeit she ribbed him at times, but Ross knew what he was about. He would come up with something different. Ross did all that computer stuff that she hated. He could run through profiles, but he can also take a lead when she charged. Yes, she liked Als and was certainly happier working with him. Where on earth had Macleod got Patterson from?*

They travelled back into Stornoway, and Clarissa decided she needed some lunch before they returned to the station. Sitting in one of the local supermarket's cafe, she ate her way through a pasty and sat in silence with Patterson beside her.

The man ate a cheese sandwich as if it was a gourmet delight, savouring it, cutting it up into small pieces, and followed it up with a bottle of water. Clarissa sat with a rather disappointing coffee. 'I'm going to need a few groceries before we get back to the station,' she said.

'Like what?' asked Patterson.

'Personal things, okay? Personal things.'

Personal things that came as white tablets; paracetamol. Her head was pumping. She stood up and went back into the store proper and looked for paracetamol. As she passed one aisle, she saw Angus Burns still in this boiler suit, but with a shopping trolley in front of him.

'That's Angus Burns,' she said to Patterson.

'Yes, it is,' came the dry reply.

'Which elder was he in the church?'

'Well, some of the other people said he was quite senior, didn't they?'

'One of the top two, wasn't it?' said Clarissa.

'Yes, that's correct. So?'

'So, if there was anything at the core of this, he would've known about it. He either covered it up, or he moved somebody on, right?' She turned around and marched down

159

the aisle. Patterson came flapping behind her.

As Clarissa approached Angus Burns, she saw a panicked face, and she stopped only a foot away from him, pulling out a warrant card and holding it up to his face.

'Good afternoon, Mr Burns. My name is Detective Sergeant Clarissa Urquhart. You've already met DC Patterson, and to be frank, I'm not happy with the answers you gave his questions.'

Clarissa could hear a tut from behind, but in fairness, Patterson wasn't jumping in front of her.

'I need to talk to you about Donald Anderson. A bit of trouble he had, those accusations around the boys.'

Angus Burns was looking around him now and a few heads had picked up. 'You can't talk about that sort of thing in here,' said Burns. 'That's old news. Besides, there was nothing in it.'

'There was nothing in it,' said Clarissa. 'Let's talk about it here. I want to know, what exactly were the allegations against him?'

'Well, I can't exactly remember.'

'You're an elder in a church and your minister gets accused of playing with the kids, and not in a good way, and you're telling me you can't remember? That's sounding like somebody with something to hide.'

'Shush,' said Burns. 'Keep your voice down.'

Clarissa reared up under the balls of her feet. 'I didn't think you caught who I was. Detective Sergeant Clarissa Urquhart, and I'm asking you a question, sir, and you will answer it.'

'I will not answer that question here.'

'You can answer it down the station, then. I'll make a note that you were highly uncooperative with our investigation. These things have a habit of blowing up and pulling others in.' The man was shrinking now, shoulders in tight, looking around him to see who was paying attention, and there were plenty of people paying attention.

'Can we talk about this outside?' he said.

'Only if you're going to talk to me about it and not give me the drivel you gave my constable earlier on. He's been brought up right and by the book. He'll take notes and stuff and ask polite questions. I don't.' Then Clarissa had a moment of inspiration. 'You understand if I don't get the answers, we bring Macleod over.'

Angus Burns stared at her, his face angry, but he was also afraid. She knew Macleod had come from here and because of several incidents that had happened on the island, which Macleod had got to the bottom of, he was well known. But he wasn't always well-liked amongst his people, in Clarissa's mind.

The problem was that he was no longer one of them. There was a great deal of religiosity but the thing about religiosity is every now and again, it spawns the genuine believer. Macleod was decent inside and was happy for the truth to get out whatever it was because he didn't fear it.

'We'll talk outside,' said Burns in a quiet voice. Clarissa held out an arm showing the man should lead the way, and she followed him beyond the trolley park to a smoking area corner. There was no one there, but Burns took a position as if he was about to light up.

'Okay, talk,' said Clarissa, 'and quick, otherwise we're going back in there to continue the discussion.'

'Look,' said Burns, 'there were rumours, okay? Some parents came and spoke to me. They didn't have any evidence. There was nobody that said he'd done anything particularly wrong. Just some of his actions at the time were over-friendly. I didn't

161

know if he really was or wasn't. The problem was we can't have that sort of thing. When I went to shush it up, the parents weren't for backing down, so I told the elders we had to get rid of him. We had to move him on. We didn't want to. He was a good minister, a very good minister.'

'He moved on where?'

'He's on the island. Donald changed his name to Raymond and changed his look. Went away for about three years before he came back, but I knew who he was. He doesn't live on this side of the island anymore. He's on Scalpay.'

'Do you have an address?' asked Clarissa. Burns rhymed off an address and Clarissa turned around, waving her hands at Patterson, indicating he should make a note.

'I tell you again, he did nothing. There was no evidence that he did anything wrong. I just acted to…'

'Keep the peace?' suggested Patterson.

'Exactly.'

'I thought you guys brought things out into the light. I thought there was a decency in it. Apparently not,' said Clarissa. 'Right? We're going to visit him. I'd like to say thank you for your time, Mr Burns, but frankly, I've had to chase you down. Next time a police officer speaks to you, tell him the truth.'

As Clarissa walked off towards the car, she could hear the tut of Patterson.

'I got results better than your fancy happy smile technique.'

'You were lucky.'

'I was not lucky.' Clarissa turned angrily. 'He had it in his eyes. All this stuff, all this politeness, all this ask questions like this, like that. What you haven't got yet is the experience. You don't know when to go for the jugular and it's important because some of these bastards, you can only go with the jugular. And get in the damn car.'

Clarissa climbed in, started up the engine, and spun the car quickly out of the carpark and on to the main road.

Scalpay was a good drive away. They would have to route down to Tarbert, then out on that bumpy road, the one that swung up and down all the way out to the isle. She tried to breathe easily as she drove, but the car was racing and she could see Patterson's hands going out again.

'If I crash at this speed, your arm will not stop you.'

After taking the winding and highly uneven road over to Scalpay, Clarissa and Patterson crossed the bridge that separated the small island from the main isle. She drove the car to a house on the edge beyond the main settlement. There was another car sitting in the drive and Clarissa jumped out, marching up to the door. She thumped on it, only to find it swung open.

'Donald Anderson,' she cried. 'Raymond, or whatever else you call yourself these days, this is DS Clarissa Urquhart. We need to speak to you.' There came a clatter.

'That's from the garage,' said Patterson. He turned and spun out of the door, running around to the side of the house. It was an old-style garage door with a handle that you had to turn and lift, and by the time Clarissa got there, Patterson had already heaved it up. She raced past him where she saw, swinging in the middle of the garage, a male figure. The legs were still moving, as were the arms. She flung herself, grabbing the legs and pushing upward.

'Get him down,' cried Clarissa. 'Get him down.'

Patterson grabbed a pair of stepladders from nearby and then brought out a pocketknife. The neck was cut free from

163

its bonds, and Clarissa lowered the man down to the floor. He was still gasping for however the attempt was made, it hadn't worked.

'Ambulance,' said Clarissa, 'and tell them to get uniform out here too.'

Clarissa sat him upright. 'You're okay?' She blurted at the man. 'You're okay.' Calling Patterson, they each reached under an arm and lifted the man across to the edge of the garage so he could sit upright against the wall.

Clarissa sat down beside him. 'Donald Anderson, is it you?'

'Yes,' he croaked. 'What is it you want?'

'Considering you just tried to swing from the ceiling, I think you know what it is I want. Let's talk about…'

'I did nothing. Look, I did nothing. Why do you think I live here? Why do you think I live away from everyone? Why do you think I went away? I've got a problem. Okay? Yes, I am the sick in mind. That is the way my mind goes, but I walked away from it. I walked away from it and Angus was meant to cover it up because I had done nothing. These thoughts, I haven't acted on them, but I would have. Except, I got help. I see specialists, but I keep myself to myself and I keep away. Understand?'

'Okay,' said Clarissa. 'Why hang yourself?'

'When Angus rang, I thought it was coming. I thought there'd be press, everything. Look, I can live with myself because I have done nothing, but I know I need to live away from others because of what goes on up here.' He pointed to his head. 'It's not good, but I have done nothing.'

Clarissa sat beside the man as they waited for the ambulance. Why would this be a problem for those people? They were carrying out the other killings. Would they come for this guy?

164

He said he had done nothing. Clearly, there had been an issue. Clearly, he had been on the cusp of things, but he'd gone away and got help. Was she looking at a smoke screen? Was she looking at a way for the investigation to be derailed, to be pushed into some other corner? She'd need to talk to Seoras. He would know.

'I hate to tell you, Mr Anderson, that you're currently in the middle of a much bigger plot. We're going to put someone on you for your safety. I'll explain a bit more in detail once the medics have checked you out.'

Clarissa had stood up once the medics arrived and walked to the edge of the garden of the house. It looked out towards the Minch, which separated Lewis and Harris from the mainland. Eric Patterson approached her from behind.

'He could have been dead.'

'Yes, he could,' said Clarissa, 'but we got here. People were hiding something. Sometimes you must push. Sometimes you have to rattle the cage.'

'But you could have ended up with a body in your hands.'

'That's the trouble with secrets,' said Clarissa. 'Don't keep them. They end up killing people. If they had kept none of this secret, the man might have got better help, or indeed, at that time, they might have just thrown him out in that Minch.'

Patterson shook his head and walked off towards the green sports car. *Not sure he's a long-term partner*, thought Clarissa. *Probably not.*

Chapter 19

Hope could see the lights of Edinburgh over the bridge, still lit although it was early morning. Soon they'd disappear, and she'd have to wake her colleague beside her. Susan Cunningham had slept ever since they left Inverness. She was in a rather awkward position, one leg up across the knee of the other, twisted slightly, and her long blonde hair wrapped around her face. Hope found it quite funny.

When she got into the car, although tired, she looked like this blonde bombshell ready to take on the world. Now she looked like a slightly old teenager, twisted up in the car seat, mouth open, drool falling to one side. Hope remembered the days when she could sleep like that. Not anymore. Now she wanted a proper bed. Now she wanted John.

She gave him a ring on the car phone as she travelled down. It was the middle of the night, but she knew she'd done the right thing when he talked to her for at least twenty minutes without her speaking back. Seoras had rung, but John was still edgy. She forgot sometimes that it wasn't normal for other people to find dead bodies. Certainly not at their place of work.

Despite the desire to get back to him, to hold him and take

on his burdens, Hope knew where she was needed. Seoras had given her pretty much free rein to run the team, and now suddenly he was putting the foot down, organising. She couldn't see it now, but she feared this was going to be much bigger than what they were doing now. That was the thing about Seoras, that experience, experience she was slowly gaining. His ability to see the bigger picture so early, and to discover what was really going on.

Hope tapped her companion on the shoulder as they entered the edge of Edinburgh and made for the university campus. It was spread out, so Hope headed for the main records office and watched as she drove, Cunningham taking various baby wipes to her face.

'I've got a bag under this eye,' she said, looking into the small cosmetic mirror in the sun visor of the car.

'I wouldn't get that worried about it,' said Hope. 'You really don't have to worry about looks.'

'Can I ask a question?'

'Sure.'

'That scar on your cheek, somebody told me you got that from an acid burn.'

'That's correct,' said Hope. 'I was stopping an attacker going after Seoras's partner.'

'He must really like you then.'

'The boss?' smiled Hope. 'The boss likes everybody. You've just got to get to know him.'

'Did you ever think of covering it up?'

'The scar?' queried Hope. 'Why? Why would I cover the scar up?'

'Well, you know, I mean, men will notice it. You don't mind me saying.'

'Saying what?'

'Well, you're tall, you're six foot, you're a redhead. I mean, look at you. You've got everything going in that department. Why not get a bit of cosmetic surgery?'

'Because this is me. This is me,' said Hope. 'I don't march around trying to please everybody else with how I look. I have a man and he looks, and he enjoys me, as I do him. He's not put off by the scar. Don't pander to people like that,' said Hope. 'I'm not telling you who you should go with or anything like that, but if all you've got is your looks to sell, then you'll end up with somebody that just wants looks.'

'Somebody said to me I was on the team because I would compliment the boss. He's grumpy and I would look good on the telly.'

'You got picked by Seoras. Seoras doesn't pick people lightly. Seoras and I are two very different people, but we've learned from each other, we've developed. If there's one thing I know about him, he'll have picked you for your ability, not for your looks. Seoras picked nobody to please the press or anyone else. Seoras only ever picked someone to get to the bottom of a case and I'll tell you, for now, this reputation you've got…'

'What reputation?' interrupted Susan.

'Reputation of being easy,' said Hope. 'Sorry if that offends you, but that's the reputation you have. He would not like that reputation. That goes against the time he grew up in. It's up to you who you want to sleep with and what you do, but Macleod wouldn't like that one, so he must have picked you because he thought you were good. He's put you with me because I had the same trouble when I was younger. People would try to put me in places for how I look, but Seoras saw me for what I could do. So have a little trust in your abilities, not in how you look, and by the way, bags will come under the eyes whatever you do.'

Hope drove the car up onto the campus, realising that this was one of her first-ever pep talks. She was slightly mortified having given it, but Cunningham seemed receptive.

'We go to records, we ask to see if anybody was about when this lot were at university, find someone who might know them.'

The young man at the records desk was extremely helpful once Hope produced a warrant card. He scanned into the records and then did a crosscheck to see if anybody was still here who would've been around at that time. It took him a minute, but then he brought Hope around to look at the screen on the computer.

'One of our librarians would've been there. In fact, she's shown as being in one of the clubs. I don't know what the club is. It says Exploration. Sigma Exploration. I don't know what that is, but you can ask her. She'll be up at the main library. She's quite high up now, one of our main librarians, Margaret Thompson. If you go up there and ask for her, I'm sure Margaret will fill you in about these people.'

Hope and Susan made their way across campus, coming to the main library and asking at the desk if Margaret Thompson was available. Hope was slightly shocked when a woman came down dressed in smart black shoes, a long skirt nearly down to her ankles, and a rather bland blouse. Her black hair was short and there was very little colour about the woman. She was pale, but she gave a faint smile as Hope approached.

'I'm Detective Inspector Hope McGrath and this is Detective Constable Susan Cunningham. We'd like to talk to you, Margaret Thompson, about some people you were possibly friends with a long time ago. It may be best if we get a room.'

'Of course,' said the woman, 'come this way.'

Hope and Susan were given seats beside a large window that looked out over the campus. Hope glanced at the students going here and there and thought that Susan wouldn't look out of place. Although Hope nowadays would probably be more like the staff than the students.

'What is it I can help you with?' asked Margaret, placing a cup of tea in front of Hope and another one in front of Susan. She then sat down, crossed one leg, and sipped her tea while Hope spoke.

'I believe you were in a group called Sigma Exploration back in the day. I know that's many years ago, but I'd like to hear about it and about certain people within it, namely Derek Clark, Ellie Fraser, and Hugh Barkley.'

Hope wouldn't have believed that the woman's face could have gone paler, but it did.

'You know them then?' asked Susan.

'Yes,' said the woman. Her teacup rattled on the saucer as she held it underneath.

'Bad memories?' asked Hope.

'Not good. You may find it difficult to believe, Inspector, but back in my day, I was a bit of a wild child. I hadn't long started working here, and I wasn't an academic from birth. I didn't get the qualifications, but I got work as a junior librarian. Hugh Barkley took a shine to me and asked if I wanted to join his group, and I did for maybe nine months.'

'But?' asked Hope.

'Well, he was very hedonistic. They all were, and it was that time when people were experimenting. At the start we'd experiment with drugs, experiment with beer, and then he wanted to experiment sexually. I was up for it, I have to say, and mostly, in the beginning, it was fun. Different partners, different positions, things that were a little wild and wacky. We read that *Kama Sutra* book, things like that. I know you're looking at me now and thinking how on earth, but well, we all go downhill after our youth, don't we?'

Yes, thought Hope, *we do*.

'The thing was that after maybe four or five months, he got into things that were a bit more forced. He became an abuser. He also started recruiting a lot of younger men and women. The ages were getting younger. Everyone was eighteen, at least among the students, but then other people came in. People from the street. People I didn't know. It all got weird.

'They had toys, as they called them, items, but to be truthful with you, I left. I enjoyed the freedom aspect, but when it turned into something that was abusive, well, I wasn't for that. I know I don't look like much, but I am a strong person, and I wouldn't take that sort of thing from anyone, so I left the group.'

'But the group continued?' asked Susan.

'Yes. You would've been ideal for him. He'd have liked you, but he also liked men. Back then, of course, that wasn't a done thing, though I had no problem with that side of it. It's the abuse that went on afterwards. I heard from others who had been in the group. In whispered conversations, they admitted people were having things done to them they shouldn't. They weren't getting a choice. Younger people were being brought in.'

'Did nobody act on that knowledge?' asked Hope.

'Well, yes, they looked into it, the university, but they couldn't find anything out. There was nobody coming forward to say anything. Eventually, the group disbanded, but their names were known.'

'Who else was in the group?' asked Susan.

'You've got three of the main characters. They were the leaders, along with Patricia Henderson and George Pole. George was the one I liked, although back then he went with whoever, whenever. Like I say, a different time, not something I'm very proud of for where it went.'

'Do you know what happened to any of these people? Because three of them have ended up in the clergy.'

'No, I don't. I mean, you can check the university records, but we don't really keep great tabs on where people have gone unless they have fed us that information. Come with me and I'll try to find out for you.'

After finishing their tea, Hope and Susan were taken along to Margaret's office. She sat behind a computer searching through alumni records and awards of degrees.

'If they became vicars and took a divinity degree, it wasn't done here in Edinburgh,' said Margaret. 'All I've got is them all finishing. Finishing well, too. All of them passed. There's no slight in their record. In fact, nowadays, beyond the likes of me and maybe a few of the older lecturers, nobody's going to remember. Did you say you were pursuing them, or they were dead?'

'They're dead,' said Hope. 'Was there anyone, particularly on the campus, you can recall who felt abused by them?'

'No. Like I say, that came afterwards. I knew most of the people from the university who were in the group, but they brought these people in from elsewhere, younger people. At least that's what I heard. The first time they did it and the younger person walked in, I walked out. So I'm sorry I can't help you there.'

Hope left the university building and sat on a bench outside amongst trees and grassland.

'Don't we need to get going?' asked Susan.

'I've driven all night and I've just heard a ton of information,' said Hope. 'I need to stop. Coffee shop. I can see it. About a hundred yards away. Cappuccino, please.'

Susan shook her head, disappeared off, and came back with a coffee for Hope, and a large frappe for herself. Hope looked at the iced drink and thought to herself that was going to need to change. Seoras didn't do frappes.

'So, Susan, what did you make of that?'

'Well, you can see why someone wanted them dead if that's the sort of thing they were getting up to. Nothing to prove, nothing to bring up, and there were five of them, so we need to look for Patricia Henderson and George Pole.'

'Yes, we do. We give that to Ross. What else do we need to do?'

'Well, while we're here, I guess we could look into records, newspaper records, things like that.'

'Good idea. Until we know where these people are, we either need to be of use here, or we need to get back up to Inverness and base. Phone it into Seoras,' said Hope.

'Shouldn't you do that? You're the Inspector, after all.'

'Tell him I'm asleep, catching forty winks because I drove all night, letting you snooze off.'

'I don't think that's a good idea. I mean, he'll be thinking I've not done my bit.'

'No, he won't,' said Hope. 'He caught me last night, said you were tired, said you weren't up to the pace of this yet. But you will be, so phone him and tell him. We're one team, Susan.

Don't worry about what he thinks of you. If it's bad, you'll
know. He'll tell you to your face.'

Chapter 20

Macleod had a fitful night and had stayed in the office, popping down occasionally to see how Ross had been getting on. The previous day had been eventful, but not so much as the morning that came after the night. He'd seen Hope disappear off to Edinburgh with Cunningham. Capturing a couple of hours' sleep, he spent another hour working through ideas of what was going on.

He popped down to the main office, encouraging those working through the night. Ross looked tired, but the man was a genius at coordinating things. Macleod had also popped down to see Jona Nakamura, the forensic lead, but there were no further clues as to the attackers. Somebody was teaching them how to work spotlessly. Only Hope's grab for an escaping leg showed as a moment when they might have got them, or at least broken into the circle.

She would come up with more. That was the trouble with Hope; she was never convinced she would come up with it, and yet she did. Sure, Ross could search through this and that, but Hope's dogged work usually came up with something.

He also had a fretful moment thinking about the poor Isle of Lewis getting Clarissa tearing through it. Part of him wanted to go back just to see the place he grew up, for he still had a fondness for it. He still remembered the bogland, the trees around the castle grounds, and the water. The comforting water, out where his first wife lay, deep in the entrance to Stornoway Harbour. But he needed to manage from here. He needed to control the game and send his players out. He was worried about Clarissa, though.

She'd reacted badly to seeing Derek Clark. While he didn't blame her for that, it had slightly knocked his confidence in the relationship she was going to build up with the new DC, Eric Patterson. He could see no such problems with Hope and Susan. But Eric, clever as he was, needed to see some reality about the police work. There was nothing more brutal than Clarissa on form. Unfortunately, she wasn't on form. Maybe she was slightly reckless at the moment. If Ross was with her, he could have tamed that. He'd have stepped in when there was an issue, but now, he wasn't so sure Eric would do that.

When Susan rang in just before lunchtime, he took the information about the potential other members of the Sigma Exploration Group and passed it to Ross. The younger man started searching up Patricia Henderson and George Pole, starting with their university records, to see where they'd gone. He scanned through churches and other religious organisations, seeing as three of the group had found their way there.

After lunch, Macleod descended to find Ross looking rather excited.

'Sir, we've got him. George Pole's a minister in a Methodist Church. Well, he was. He's now retired, lives in Braemar. I've contacted the local police to see if they can find him.'

'Anything more, though? What about Patricia Henderson?'

'Nothing at the moment,' said Ross. 'I'll keep you informed.'

Macleod retired back up to his office and, because he was at a loss for what else to think about, was going through some paperwork when Ross called him back down again.

'Flower house, sir. Flower house,' said Ross excitedly.

'What's Flower House?'

'The letters that Steven saw out the window. Flower House, W-E-R H-O, flower house.'

'There must be dozens of flower houses.'

'LNBO.'

'LNBO?'

'Delnabo.'

'Delnabo?' queried Macleod.

'There's no word like Delnabo. I can't find any other words like it. It's Flower House Delnabo. I've gone on Google Maps,' said Ross. 'That's where he was held, just across from it. I'm sure there's a signpost you can see from the other house.'

'Two minutes, Ross, out the back with me.'

Macleod ran up the stairs, shouted to the secretary he was out, and grabbed his coat. He didn't wait for a reply and was down in the car waiting for Ross. The younger man jumped into the driver's seat.

'Sorry, sir.'

'Don't be sorry, Ross, let's go.' Macleod's phone rang as Ross started the engine.

'Clarissa. You're what?'

Clarissa was on the end of the phone, advising that Donald Henderson was now living on Scalpay. He'd also just tried to kill himself. Macleod listened as she spat out the information.

'This sounds like a smoke screen. We're on route to the house. Ross has cracked the letters Stephen saw. Flower House in

177

Delnabo.'

'What do you want me to do?' asked Clarissa.

'Stay over there. Make sure there's somebody on Donald Henderson. I think it's a smoke screen, just meant to make people think it's about us, about me, about the police not getting something right. From what you say, Henderson did nothing. There's no victim with Henderson because he enacted nothing. He's a sad case, and it's not right, but it's not fitting those getting killed. In case I'm wrong, stay over there. I'll talk to you further once we get to Delnabo.'

Ross raced along the A9 heading south before cutting off towards Delnabo. It was a tiny village with only a few houses. As they got closer, Ross pulled up short of the property.

Together, Ross and Macleod stared at the property from a hedge near the roadside. To get close was going to be awkward, but Macleod wanted to know if somebody was there.

'If we can get in and have a look without alerting them to the fact that we actually know where this is, we may see if they're still using it. Because if they are, we might trap them,' said Macleod. 'Let's try to get a sneaky look.'

'We go over there, sir,' said Ross. 'Come in past that hedge. That's the shortest run toward the house. We'll have to go through that other house's grounds. That's Flower House. We go through there and that will be the house Steven was being held in.'

Together, the two of them fought their way past the hedge and entered the grounds of Flower House. Macleod rapped on the door, and it was opened by a young man. Macleod told him that whatever was about to happen, he was to stay put in the house. If he saw anything untoward, he was to call the police. Carefully, Ross and Macleod went out of the rear garden of the house and reached a hedge that separated it from the building that Steven had been held in. It was a barbed wire fence. Slowly, they picked their way over it and then crouched down, ready for a sprint.

'If there's someone in, what do we do?' asked Ross.

'If we can, subdue them, but if it's dangerous, we fall back, we block the road out and we call back up in.'

'Okay,' said Ross. 'You ready?'

'I'm not that old, Ross,' said Macleod. 'Of course, I'm ready.'

However, in his head, he wished he had Hope here, and maybe Cunningham and Patterson too. In fact, Clarissa wouldn't have been a terrible choice. She fought dirty, but she fought well. But there was nothing for it. It was time to go.

'When you're ready, Ross,' said Macleod.

Ross was up and away before Macleod had even finished the sentence and he tailed in his wake. Ross had got three-quarters of the way there before the front door opened and a man ran out, screaming at them. In his right hand, he held a machete. Ross went to turn away, but the man was quick, closing in on him and swiped down with the blade.

Ross put his hands up and blocked the first blow. The man was good with the weapon and rolled it back off Ross's defences and swiped in again, hacking into the back of Ross's thigh.

Ross screamed and Macleod could see blood soaking in through his trouser leg. The man reached up again and came down with another blow, but Ross had put his hands up and caught the man's wrist. Macleod was getting closer now. The maniac hadn't focused on him and was looking to bring the blade down on top of Ross again. Macleod barrelled into him, shoulder first, hitting the guy just above the hip and knocking him sideways.

Together, the two of them rolled. Knowing that the man had a large knife, Macleod rolled away from him as quick as he could, before getting back up on his feet. He felt his shoulder ache. He felt his legs wobble slightly, but he focused as best as he could on the man with the blade coming towards him.

Ross was screaming. Macleod bent down, his right hand finding gravel. He stood up slowly as the man approached quickly. Macleod threw a handful of gravel straight into the man's face. There was dust with it, and he was momentarily blinded.

Macleod's hands shot to the man's wrist and then he kicked the back of the man's leg as hard as he could. The man toppled forward. Macleod drove the wrist down towards the ground. The blade was released, and Macleod followed down with his entire weight onto the man's back.

Ross had one hand clamped around his leg, but he was sliding himself over. With his free hand, he grabbed the man's wrist, holding him, allowing Macleod to reach around and grab the handcuffs. He snapped them on the man's wrists, keeping the arms behind the man's back.

Ross was shouting, telling Macleod to phone for an ambulance. Ross had also manoeuvred himself, so he now lay on top of the man. The man was struggling, but Macleod stood on top of him, planting a boot between the man's shoulders.

Macleod dialled, but there was no signal. *Blast it*, he thought. He looked over at the house they'd come from. At the window was the man they had spoken to earlier. Macleod waved his phone at the man, pointing to it, and got a thumbs-up back.

It took twenty minutes before the first squad car arrived. By that point, Macleod had kicked the man in the back several times, telling him to stop moving. He'd also applied half of his jacket around Ross's leg, tying it up as tight as he could. The ambulance arrived five minutes later. Macleod sat on the ground while the paramedics attended to Ross.

'Sorry,' said Ross as he was being lifted into the ambulance.

'Don't be,' said Macleod. 'You guys take good care of him. I need him.'

Macleod was annoyed with himself. These people were killers. The fact they'd let Steven go had almost made them seem reasonable. Macleod had got overexcited. He had thought there was something here, believed he could set a trap, and now one of his most important people was off in an ambulance. The cut had looked deep, and there was plenty of blood. As the ambulance departed, Macleod turned to the two constables who had arrived in the first police car.

'What's your names?' he said.

'Alan. This is James. We know who you are, sir.'

'It's Seoras,' he said. 'Thank you,' and he put his hand out, shaking theirs. 'I need a little help. We're going to search this house. You with me?'

'Yes, Seoras,' said Alan, and followed him in. The house was pretty bare. There was a kitchen with a small amount of food. There were some sleeping bags, but only one seemed to be used at the moment, the rest stashed away. Whoever this figure was, Macleod would have to interrogate him to find out who the others were.

In one room at the rear, however, stood several cardboard boxes. Macleod put on some gloves and opened them. As he looked inside, his mind boggled.

'Guys,' he said. 'Do any of you know what this is for?'

181

'Well, they look like sex aids of some sort,' said Alan. 'I've not got experience myself, but they look…'

'They look quite severe, don't they?' said Macleod. 'As I understand it, and I don't understand a lot, these are on the extreme side. Some of this would hurt, wouldn't it?'

'Oh, yes,' said Alan. 'I would say that would hurt.'

Macleod stepped away and then marched back to the squad car, where he was able to patch a call through to Jona Nakamura. He asked her to send someone down to check on the items they'd discovered. *So, this has been a base*, thought Macleod. *This is where they'd operated from or where they're still operating from. Would people come back?*

He got hold of a sergeant who had just arrived, telling him to keep an eye out on the roads for anyone returning. He wanted the scene secured for Jona's team, but what he needed to do was to talk to this attacker. The attacker had gone off in a squad car to be processed back up in Inverness, but Macleod knew that was his next place to go. As he went to turn away, Alan, the PC who had searched the house with him, came running out holding something in a gloved hand.

'Seoras,' he said, 'I think you want to see this.'

'Where'd you find that?'

'Hidden behind the chimney. Don't think the fire's been lit. There are a couple of electric bar heaters, but in this weather, you will need nothing.'

Macleod put some gloves on and set the book down on the squad car bonnet. He flicked it open and saw a myriad of numbers and letters all in large tables. It was a codebook, but for what and for who? *It was breaking*, thought Macleod, *it's breaking. Finally, we're getting somewhere. But a code book amongst four people?* He needed to talk to his attacker; he needed to understand how big this was.

Chapter 21

Hope had made the executive decision to drive towards Braemar. She knew that George Pole had retired there, and Hope had dispatched the local police to find him, but so far there'd been no report. Hope was going to get some sleep, but instead, she sat in the car letting Susan drive while she half dozed on the way up. As they cleared Perth, Hope received a call from Macleod.

'Hope, where are you? You still in Edinburgh?'

'No, I started driving back up heading towards Braemar. Have heard nothing from the local police. Have you?'

'No,' he said. She could detect a tone in his voice. He was down. 'What's up?' she asked.

'We went to Flower House in Delnabo, and we've been attacked. Ross is in hospital.'

'How serious?'

'He'll be okay. It's serious, but he'll survive. We got attacked by a man with a machete. I'm going to interview him now. We've been cleaning him up, checking him over medically, and then I should be able to get in with him.'

'Have you been to see Ross yet?' asked Hope.

'No,' said Macleod. 'I need to chase this down. He's okay.

He'll be fine. We need to focus on…'

'What is it?' asked Hope. 'What happened?'

'I told you.'

'Seoras, it's me. There's that sound in your voice.'

'I thought we could get into the place, search it on the quiet in case they were still using it. They could've been, but it was a bad call. They saw us approaching the house, or rather, he did. There was only one of them there. He came out with a machete and Ross didn't have anywhere really to go. He was on him quickly. Could have gone a lot worse, Hope. Could have gone a lot worse. Bad call.'

'Well, shake it off,' said Hope. 'Clarissa's struggling with seeing that body. We've got new people on the team. We need you on form, so shake it off. He's going to be fine. It's all part and parcel. You know that.'

'Of course I do. It's just, well…'

'You nearly lost him before, I know. I was there when he got shot in that helicopter. These things happen. I know you're fond of him. Just because he's the only one that calls you, sir.'

She heard Macleod chuckle. That was a good sign because that's what he needed, to be brought back out of himself. Not to think about this, instead to think about the case. If there was one thing the team needed, it was that brain at the top pulling it all together.

'I'll go kick arse up in Braemar,' said Hope. 'What about Clarissa? Can you pull her back?'

'I will do, but she's got to catch the ferry. Be a while before she's back. That's all a smokescreen over there. They played us, like when they left the body in the car from John's hire firm, by sending cards to a former policeman. It's all an act to drag us away. It's got Clarissa away now when I could do with her

185

here. There's something more behind this, Hope. This isn't just some simple revenge. There's something going on. I know it, and I can't think what.'

'You will,' said Hope. 'You'll get there. Now, focus. I'll call you when I find out what's happening in Braemar.'

Hope closed the call, turned to Susan and said, 'Put the foot down. We're in a hurry. And stick the light up.'

Susan switched on the blue lights and they raced up towards Braemar. *Was it strictly necessary?* Thought Hope. *Well, let's see.*

They closed off the blue lights by the time they reached Braemar and met up with the local uniform at the petrol station.

'What we got so far?' Hope asked the local sergeant.

'Tried knocking on his door. Nobody's seen him. Don't believe he's in the house. Tried the neighbours. Some aren't in. Most say they're not sure who he is exactly.'

'Have you gone into the house?' asked Hope.

'I don't have cause to,' said the sergeant, 'or do we?'

'I think we do,' said Hope. 'He's on a list of people being killed. Therefore, we need to find him. Therefore, we need the information inside. It's okay. You carry on with the local inquiries. Cunningham and I will head in to check his house out.'

Susan Cunningham drove the pair to a small house on an estate. It looked like it could do with a good coat of paint. The door had also seen better days, but the lock was intact. Hope went round the windows trying to peer in, but thick net curtains prevented her.

'Certainly not open and bright, is it?' said Cunningham, and then looked up at the lock. 'It is locked, but it won't take much to push that in.'

'You're right,' said Hope. 'You're absolutely right.' She put her hand up and then slammed it with her other, causing the door to judder, and then it swung open. Hope stepped inside the rather depressing house and onto a carpet that, at one time, had been cream. There were cigarette burns on the floor and the entire house smelled mouldy.

'Are you sure this is the right place?' asked Susan. 'The other houses we went to, their victims were living somewhere neat. It wasn't like this.'

'No,' said Hope, 'but they're all different. They're not connected by what they love in house decor. They're connected by something very different.'

Hope walked down the hallway and opened a wooden door into a living room. The bottom of the wooden door was flaking, a cheap imitation. Inside the living room were piles of crisps packets and larger cans dumped in a corner.

'Similarly impressive in here then,' said Susan, following in behind her. She began searching through a dresser on the far side.

'You take that,' said Hope. 'I'm going to have a look upstairs.' She exited the living room and could be heard creaking all the way up the stairs until she got to the bedroom. Once up there, she found a sparse bedroom. The sheets were thrown back off the bed, and she looked through drawers with old jeans, trousers and worn jumpers. Nothing was new and pristine.

In one corner of the bedroom was a small filing cabinet. On pulling it back, Hope found lots of photographs inside. She called Susan up from downstairs. Most of the photographs had images of scantily clad men or women. Although Hope was unsure if these were men or women, or were they boys and girls? None of them were exceptionally young. Most would

187

have been in the latter half of secondary school, at the very least. But, she thought, some of them may be minors.

'What do you think?' asked Hope. 'What age would you say they were?'

'I don't know,' said Susan, 'but look at the photographs. None of them are the same. They're all taken with a camera as well. Do you think these are his own?'

'Could be,' said Hope. 'Looks like he hasn't got away from his fetish of the university years.'

'Indeed not,' said Susan. 'We need to find this guy.'

Hope continued to look through the filing cabinet and found a couple of passport-size photographs. They were located beside an application for a driving licence.

'This is him,' said Susan. 'Not the most handsome looking of men.'

He was completely bald-headed. Hope noted that it was shaved, and not from natural loss.

'You can tell because it's growing back in places. When a beard gets cut off, it comes back as stubble. It's the same for the head unless you shave it regularly, and really well.'

'I'll take your word for it,' said Susan. 'Strange look, though, especially at his age. He used to be a vicar, apparently.' The application was signed as the Reverend George Pole.

'At least we got something,' Hope said.

Susan, meanwhile, had walked to the far side of the room and started opening some other drawers. 'He's got a load of toupees in here.'

Hope marched over. The blonde-haired woman kept picking them up and putting them on her head.

'Those aren't toupees. They're wigs. He's disguising himself. This is how he's taking the photographs,' said Hope.

The women continued to search upstairs and found another room, complete with a laptop and several cameras. There was a small spy camera, bigger ones for photographing, and large, wide-angled lenses.

'It's like the pervert paparazzi, isn't it?' said Susan. 'Maybe that's why he keeps a low profile.'

They spent the next forty minutes interviewing the neighbours, all of whom said that they rarely saw the man. One mentioned he might have gone out earlier. Given that he wasn't in, this seemed reasonable to follow up on.

'Did you notice anything about him when he came out of the house, though?' asked Hope. 'Anything to show where he was going?'

'One thing,' the neighbour said, 'he was putting a glove on. It was white, and I didn't see the other one. I've never seen him put a glove on. I think he took it out of a packet. It may even have arrived this morning because I think he was ripping it open. He tried this glove on and then closed the door behind him.'

'He must have taken the rubbish with him then,' said Susan. 'There's nothing in the hall.'

'Indeed,' said Hope. 'White glove. One of. Where could he be going?'

'Unless he's doing a Michael Jackson impersonation, he's got to be off to the golf club.'

'You're right,' said Hope, pointing at Susan. 'The golf club. Where's the nearest golf club?' she asked the neighbour.

He indicated the local club was only a few miles away, and the women jumped into the car and headed there directly. The golf club was small, and the course wound up into the hills. From the clubhouse, Hope could see the first and the eighteenth hole, but little else, as the course was hidden behind trees up and down through valleys.

She approached the pro shop and found a quiet older man inside. He was dressed in a Pringle sweater and gave her a toothy grin as she approached.

'Are you two ladies looking to book a tee time? I've got to be honest; we don't get many like you around here. They don't really like the jeans either, if you're going out on the course to play.'

Hope pulled her warrant card out. 'Detective Inspector Hope McGrath, this is Detective Constable Susan Cunningham. I'm sure your course is lovely, but we're not here to do that. Do you know this man, by any chance?'

She held up one of the small passport photographs for the golf shop pro to look at.

'Yes, he's out on the course. That's Steven Jolly. Became a member a couple of years ago.'

'Does he play often?'

'Once or twice a week, always on his own. He popped in here maybe an hour and a half ago, two hours. I'd say he'd be out somewhere on the course. He never says much, but you try to get a bit of banter with your customers, don't you?'

'Sure. Have you got a course map?' asked Hope.

'Yes, I do,' said the pro. He handed the scorecard with the map on the back to Hope. 'There's a road running around the outside. If you take that, you'll get up towards nine, ten, eleven, twelve, possibly even towards thirteen. They all run up alongside the road there. That's probably your quickest way to get him. If you walk out through the course, it'll take a while. You could take a buggy, but personally, I'd take the road. It'd be quicker.'

'Did he say anything to you today?' asked Susan.

'Not much. No. In fact, no. He said one thing. That's right,' said the pro. 'He asked me how long that black van had been there.'

'What black van?' asked Hope.

'There was a black van. It'd been sitting there since about seven this morning. I don't know who it belongs to. They hadn't come in, but I remember because Steven said to me, "How long has it been there?" I said to him what I knew, and he asked if anybody had come in from it. No, I hadn't spoken to anyone from it. It was sitting there in the corner underneath the large tree.'

Susan looked over at Hope. 'No black van when I came in. Don't remember seeing it.'

She ran over to the pro shop club door, opened it, was outside for about thirty seconds, then came back in. 'No van.'

'We need to move. We'll be back,' she said to the pro and turned and burst out of the door.

'Get in the car,' said Hope. 'You drive. If they're going to grab him, they'll have to do it with the van. Obviously, he was worried. He must know the news.'

Hope slid into the passenger seat, and Susan fired up the car. Hope pointed her out of the clubhouse car park and then down the road that sped through the countryside. It brought them round amongst the trees at the edge of the course.

'You watch the road. I'll look,' said Hope, 'but keep it slow. Slow now. Come on, give me a chance.'

Hope scanned and saw a flag on a green. It was one hole and there was no one there. The next hole had a couple of women on it playing. Beyond that, there was a single man on his own. Driving up the fairway was a van.

'There,' shouted Hope, 'there.'

Susan raced along, looking for somewhere to get onto the course.

'Stop the car,' said Hope. 'You find a gap. Bring the car on.'

She slammed the door behind her, jumped across a small stream and out onto the course. The green was a good hundred yards away. She could see a man being grabbed by two people in black. They had masks on, and the man was struggling to resist.

'Police! Stop!' shouted Hope. 'Let him go.'

From out of the van, someone else emerged with a baseball bat and they ran towards Hope. She made directly for them and pulled up abruptly as they swung the bat, missing her by a mere inch. She stepped inside of them, hitting them hard on the shoulders, knocking them backwards. They recovered in time to swing the bat again.

This time, Hope could barely get out of the way and was caught on the shoulder. Her attacker didn't stop, swung the bat back and Hope ducked just in time, hearing the bat whistle past her head. She kicked out at the person's knees, and they squealed in pain, but before falling, Hope reached for the bat. Someone behind her kicked her hard in the back, just under the ribs, and she toppled forward.

She saw a woman dressed in black pick up the bat and she slammed it down on top of her. Hope winced in pain. She hoped something wasn't cracked because she got her arms just in the way of her ribs. As the woman swung down again, Hope rolled to one side. Then there came an almighty crash.

Hope rolled clear and onto her feet and she saw their car now buried in the back of the van. Susan Cunningham had stepped out and was currently taking on someone from the front of the van. He had a knife and was swinging it this way and that. Behind him, unconscious, Steven Jolly was being thrown into the back of the van by one man.

Hope was now approached again by the person with the baseball bat. Hope stepped inside of the swing and drove a hard palm of her hand up to the chin of her attacker and connected well. The attacker fell backwards, but Hope saw her colleague pinned to the ground with a knife being held over her. Rather than revisit her own attacker, she ran over, delivering a hard kick to the guts of Susan's attacker.

She put a hand down, grabbing the wrist that was holding the knife, forcing it into the ground again and again.

'They're all coming,' shouted Cunningham, getting to her feet. Hope heard a sickening thud. Cunningham cried out and then Hope felt herself being hit in the back with the baseball bat. She crumpled down and tried to wrap herself to prepare for the next blow, but none came.

As she got back vaguely upright, she saw the four black figures getting into the van. The van door closed. She heard the engine start-up. With a sickening clash of scraping metal, the van pulled away from the police car. She looked at Cunningham on the floor. The girl was woozy, extremely woozy.

'Stay there,' shouted Hope. She jumped into the car, desperate to follow as she saw the van speed off down the fairway. Hope turned the ignition. The car turned over, the engine came to life briefly. She put down the accelerator and then realised that the wheels had taken damage. As she drove off, the car limped to one side, then to the other, and then the engine threw a hissy fit and simply stopped. She tried again and again, but it wouldn't start.

Hope got out of the car and began running down the fairway after the van, before seeing it exit and come back up the road towards her location. As it sped along, she jumped out. Beneath her feet, at the stream she'd just jumped across, was a large boulder, about the size of her hand. Grabbing it, she threw it at the windscreen. Whether it was the speed of the car as it hit it or the effort of the throw, the windscreen smashed and the van swung sideways, hitting a car coming the other way. It was only a glancing blow, but it caused the van to spin.

Hope raced forward and grabbed hold of the rear door, pulling it back. Inside was a mess. Her attackers were spread all over the inside of the van, but so was Steven Jolly. She wasn't sure just how conscious he was because he was murmuring and babbling.

Hope reached in and grabbed him, pulling him out of the van. He tumbled to the floor, and she yelled as somebody hit her in the back. It was a good punch into the ribs, but she raised her elbow behind her and caught someone in the face. She dragged him forward, but there were more yells coming from outside the van.

Hope saw the baseball bat being swung at her and threw up her arms to block it. I caught her on the forearms, and she spun. She was prepared for more feet to kick her, for there were four of them. Someone stepped over the top of her and drove a punch straight into the face of the attacker with the baseball bat. The figure then turned and grabbed one attacker, trying to pull off the mask, holding them tight around the neck.

'Just get in, let's go. We've blown it. It's been blown. Let's go.'

It was a male voice, and it was deep. Hope went to stand,

but someone kicked her and then she heard Susan cry, hit again with a baseball bat. Hope flung herself over the top of Steven Jolly, determined that they'd have to pick her off before they got him, but she heard the van doors closing. The engine started again. Something was scraping as they sped away. Something in the van wasn't right, but it was disappearing at speed.

Hope looked around her. Opposite, Susan Cunningham had blood coming out of her mouth. The side of her face was coming up in a large bruise, but apart from that, Hope couldn't see any serious wounds. Steven Jolly was out for the count, but he was breathing. As for herself, her shoulder ached. Her forearms would come up in serious lumps, and she thought that one of her ribs had taken a pummelling with that punch, but she was good. She could stand, she could speak, and she could go again.

'Bloody brilliant, Susan. We got him. You hear me? We got him. You take this in because you don't always get this.'

Chapter 22

Macleod wearily trudged up the stairs to his office, where he received a rather pitiful smile from his secretary.

'Ross is doing okay, they say.'

'Did they give any more detail?' asked Macleod.

'He lost quite a bit of blood, but he's more than stable, up and talking apparently. He's got a serious wound on the leg. It's going to take him a day or so to walk, maybe a month to get fully recovered with the leg, but they reckon he could be out in a day or two. They just want to keep him in and make sure that there's nothing untoward. Apparently, he's already asking for his laptop.'

Macleod gave a wry smile. 'Anything else?'

'One of the constables downstairs wants to speak to you. One of Ross's team.'

'They'll be worried about him,' said Macleod.

'No, not that. She had information.' Macleod spun on his heel and didn't quite run down the steps, but certainly moved down them a lot quicker than he had come up. The hubbub of the office died quickly as he entered the room and he saw all eyes were on him.

'DC Ross is going to be okay. He's got a severe leg injury.

He's going to be in the hospital, so you're going to have to manage without him for a while, so feed everything through me. Okay?'

There was a sigh of relief that rippled across the room, and then a hand went up at the back.

'Carson, isn't it? Sorry, can't remember your first name,' said Macleod.

'Sandra Carson. We've just discovered something. You might need to know it, Inspector.' Macleod could see the girl was shaking as he approached, and he wondered how he did that to people.

'It's Seoras, Sandra, so if you could just tell me what you know.'

'We found Patricia Henderson. She's living in Benbecula.'

'Whereabouts?' asked Macleod. He was familiar with the area.

'Gramisdale.'

'Have you sent anyone over?'

'We sent the local police, but wondered if you thought it might be best to get someone else down there.'

'Leave it with me. Good work. Keep going on with the rest of the CCTV and all the other reports. With Ross out of the picture, I'm depending on you to keep it together.'

'Will do.' There was a pause. 'Seoras.'

'See,' he said, 'it's not that difficult, and that goes for you all,' said Macleod. 'We've got a lot of the team here, but we're everywhere, especially my inspector and my sergeant, so I need you all to keep at it. Just because they're off doing the glory hunting doesn't mean you're not important. It's a team game.'

He turned away and walked back up to his office upstairs.

He wondered if he should come down and sit in Hope's office for a while where he could look out onto the rest of the team, but he decided that was a bad idea. She was the boss from day to day down there, not him. He entered his office, picked up his phone, and called Clarissa.

'What's up?' she asked.

'We found her, Patricia Henderson. She's in Gramisdale. I'll send the address over, but you need to get booked on the ferry out of Leverburgh over to North Uist, and drive down. Local uniform has gone around to see if she's there and warn her, but I want somebody in close and I need her interviewed.'

'She shouldn't be under any threat, though, at the moment. Should she?'

'I know what you're thinking,' said Macleod, 'and you might be right. After all, Hope's just gone through a heck of a time.'

'I heard about that, and you've got the attacker to interview. We're all occupied, but I'll get on the first available down.'

'Good,' said Macleod. 'How's it working out with Patterson?'

'I rarely question what you do,' said Clarissa.

'I'm sorry,' said Macleod. 'You what?'

'I don't often question what you do, but we may not be the perfect match.'

'Just make sure you pass something onto him in your time together. If it's not working out, we're moving you on the next case we pick up.'

'How is Als?'

'Ross's going to be okay,' said Macleod. 'He took a severe blow from a machete to his leg. We stopped the guy and we've got him in custody. Ross will be a couple of days in the hospital, probably. Although they reckon he'd be up on his leg in a day or two, able to walk but probably a full month before he gets total recovery.'

'That's good,' said Clarissa. 'I was…'

'You were worried about him. I know, I do too, but he's fine. Get that ferry booked and get down there.'

Clarissa closed the call and Macleod sat back in his office chair. It often happened like this. You were getting nowhere, and the team was fine. Suddenly you were getting somewhere, and the team was getting taken down under pressure. He could hear it in Clarissa's voice. That's why Patterson was there. He was steady. That's what all the reports about him said. A very steady individual. Macleod hoped so.

* * *

Hope McGrath sat across the table from Steven Jolly in Braemar Police Station. The man was visibly shaking, but he was okay. If they hadn't rescued him, who knew what state he would've been in? The door opened behind her, and Susan Cunningham placed a mug of coffee beside Hope and then one for Steven Jolly, before sitting down herself. She had a can of cola. When she cracked it open, a 'pfft' broke the silence.

'Mr Jolly, if you can just confirm for me, you originally were George Pole.'

'That's correct,' he said. 'I was born George Pole, but I changed my name fairly recently to Steven Jolly. I'm, well, you can see what I am.'

'You were at university with Hugh Barkley, Ellie Fraser, and Derek Clark. Also Patricia Henderson, I believe.'

'All true,' said Steven Jolly. 'The days I've tried to forget about.'

'In what way?'

199

'When I went to university,' said Steven, 'I was very green, wide-eyed, thinking this is a chance to experience life. But all it did was awaken a dark side in me.'

'How so?' asked Susan.

'Well, I got on with my studies. I was an engineer, but I found myself liking younger people. When I say younger, I don't mean children. I mean those in their teens, mid-teens onwards, but not of an age when you should be with them. I thought nothing of it. Instead, I joined the group.

'It was Hugh that got me involved. I met him in a bar one night and we were eyeing up some women. I realised that we might have wanted something a bit more exciting. Well, that's what it seemed like. We got together, and with several others, we carried out what might have been termed swinging back in the day.

'Nothing particularly wrong with it. We were all consenting adults trying things out. Then the things we tried out got more and more extreme. Of course, some of us didn't like it inflicted on us, so we expanded the group. We were bringing young people in. It was very wrong. We paid them, but quite what we did was…, it wasn't right, and we all knew it, but we all couldn't get enough of it.

'When we got to the end of university with a number having left the group, we went into what can only be described as guilt. I was writing to the others; they were responding to me. We needed to do something, and we needed to be somewhere we could hide. I don't know if you can understand that.'

'So, you went to the church?' asked Hope.

'Yes, you can hide in the church. We went and got Divinity degrees, all of us. And then all to different churches. We wrote to each other in the interim. The others, they seem to have done all right. They seem to have kept off it. I haven't.'

'We got to see inside your house. You've at least kept up the practice in a photographic sense.'

'I'm ill. There's something wrong with me. I can't help it. It's not good and thank God I have touched no one since, but yes, it's not good. I invented Steven Jolly to be different. He's my alter ego, my better self, but I slipped back. I need help.'

He leaned forward onto the table and was suddenly sobbing into it.

'Do you remember the names of the young people you used?' asked Susan.

The head lifted for a moment and was shaking in a negative response.

'When you acquired them, who acquired them?'

'It was Hugh. I was out with him on occasions, but mainly they were off the street. Sure, some came back repeatedly looking for the money, but it wasn't worth what we did to them. A lot of them were struggling, though. Lived out there on the street, needed it. They had no choice, and we exploited them. Oh, dear God, we exploited them.' He bent down again.

'So far, they've come for you. They've also come for three of your fellow members of that group,' said Hope. 'What I can't believe is how well you stayed undercover, especially nowadays, with so many things being raked up.'

'We did nothing within the church. The bad times were all within the university,' said Steven. 'But more than that, it was under the radar. There was nothing to find. There were no traces.'

'Except for those that you violated,' said Susan. 'They're still about. Clearly, they haven't got over it, whoever these people are.'

'You should have let them take me. It's no more than I deserve,' said Steven.

'Have you seen anything unusual in the last couple of weeks? Anybody standing out?' asked Hope.

'No,' said Steven. 'I try to be reclusive. I go out with my name to golf, but I usually play golf on my own. The only person I really speak to is the pro.'

'Have you changed anything that you've done before?' asked Susan. 'Any routine change this week? Have you been forced off normal habits?'

'No,' said Steven, 'I've not noticed anybody. They'll come for me again, won't they?'

'I can't be certain,' said Hope, 'but maybe. We'll keep you in protective custody for the moment.'

She stepped out of the room with Susan Cunningham and they walked to the rear of the police station. There, in the light breeze that was blowing, Hope looked at Susan.

'How do they do it?'

'What do you mean?' asked Susan.

'Think about this. How do they do it? He has seen nobody about. Somebody must have been watching him. The timescale is not great. It's short. If it's just the four of them and they're hopping from here to there, they're going at an incredible rate,' said Hope. 'You've also got Delnabo. You'll be racing back and forward from it. I'm betting if we see a black van again, it will not be damaged. I know they've been burning them, but where do they get them all? They've all bought the same.'

'You think there's more than the four of them?'

'Well, there's five, at least,' said Hope. 'After all, Macleod was attacked.' Hope picked up her phone and called the station.

'It's Macleod.'

'Seoras, it's Hope. I spoke to Steven Jolly.'

'Who?'

'George Pole changed his name by deed poll to Steven Jolly, trying to make a new life. He's openly admitted to me all the acts that they did back in university. They picked up young people, not children, he said. He described them as late teenagers, but he said that they paid them. Kids off the street, and they did certain things with them, lewd acts, acts that the rest of them didn't want visited on themselves. That's why the group grew. It started off as a mutual thing, but then they needed others to do these acts upon because none of them were willing to receive them. That's probably why they're being attacked. Revenge.'

'Okay,' said Macleod. 'We've got Clarissa on her way down to Benbecula. Hopefully, she'll be able to pick up Patricia Henderson. After that, the circle's complete as far as I understand it.'

'Indeed,' said Hope, 'but what's bothering more Seoras is the fact that Steven Jolly saw no one monitoring him, never saw a black van until today. Meanwhile, we have this snatch squad running around. They take our victims, then dispatching them somewhere else before dumping them back. Awful lot of work across a massive piece of the country. I've got a bad feeling about this.'

'You think there's a lot more out there? You think there's not just one team?' said Macleod.

'That's right.'

'I've come to the same conclusion from a different angle, but there are not a lot of places to go. I don't see what their agenda's going to be once they've got rid of all five perpetrators.

How many kids did they violate? How many are coming back seeking vengeance?'

'It could be families as well, though,' said Hope. 'Well, we've got Steven Jolly in custody. We'll keep him secure, certainly until we find our killers.'

'Hopefully, I'll get into that. I'm about to talk to Peter Samson. That's my attacker in Delnabo.'

'What do you want me to do?' asked Hope.

'Tidy up down there and just stay. See if you can get any more detail on the black van. After all, you damaged it badly. It must be somewhere. See if you can find them before they go to ground.'

'Will do, Seoras. We're nearly there.'

'I hope so,' said Macleod.

Chapter 23

Macleod stood up from behind his desk, ready to descend the stairs down to the interview room to talk to Peter Samson. As he did, his secretary knocked on the door and entered.

'It's your post for the afternoon,' she said, and handed over several envelopes. Macleod looked at one. It was brown. It looked identical to those being received by the care homes.

'When did this come in?' he said to Lorraine.

'Normal post. Look, it's got a stamp on it.'

Macleod tore open the envelope. He pulled out a card inside. He heard a gasp from Lorraine, and he stared at the image on the front of the card. There was a pole, and it was rooted up inside a person, a man, and through his front genitalia. Macleod turned and placed the card down on his desk, grabbed an evidence bag before placing the card inside. Clearly, the fate for Steven Jolly had been decided, albeit that the card had been delayed in the post. Maybe it was meant to arrive yesterday.

'Do you want me to contact anyone about this?' asked Lorraine.

'Phone down to forensics. Ask Jona to get someone to come and pick it up. I've seen all I need, but don't touch it. Just leave it there in the evidence bag. You can let them into my office when they come.'

Macleod went to walk off, but then stopped. 'Are you okay?' he asked Lorraine.

'Yes,' she said after a moment. 'Just a bit of a shock seeing something like that.'

Macleod thought how badly he must have been affected throughout his career, that he looked at an image like that and didn't even flinch.

'Yes, it can get you like that. Try not to think any more about it, but if it comes back, let me know.'

He resumed his passage through the door, down the stairs, and along to the interview room, where a constable sat with Peter Samson. Macleod noted the man was handcuffed and asked in the constable's ear why this was. He said that Samson had tried to attack several people, and Macleod decided against asking for coffee during the interview.

'Peter Samson,' said Macleod, 'You attacked my officer and me with a machete. What were you doing in that house?'

The man spat across the table at Macleod. Macleod reached up, wiped it down off his cheek, and glared at the man. 'Why did you attack us?' he said calmly.

'Why do you do it?' said Samson. 'Why do you protect them? They deserve what they got. They deserve it.'

Macleod could see needle marks along the man's arm. He was clearly a junkie of some sort, but what would have taken him to that point?

'Do you know the people you're killing, or your friends are killing? It's not just you, is it? We know you held the young kid there. Steven identified certain letters of the house across from you. You see, you let him look out the window. That's how we came to be with you, but the others have left now, leaving you to take the blame. Where are they?'

'They are where they need to be. Surprised you haven't heard yet.'

'Well, I've heard. We stopped them.'

The man's face became angry. 'You stop there. You don't deal with this stuff and then you prevent us from dealing with it.'

'What stuff?' asked Macleod.

'Do you know what they did to me?' said the man. He was shaking now. 'You know what they did to me? I haven't been able to…' He looked slightly embarrassed.

'Been able to what?' asked Macleod. He could see the constable sitting beside him was getting uncomfortable.

'I haven't been able to be with anyone.'

'What did they do to you?'

'They showed me it all. You think of any sick, perverted way you can be with a person, and they showed me it. They would take items and thrust them down my throat and into all our orifices. They brutalised me and all for fun, all for experimentation, all for twenty quid.'

'Twenty quid a time? I guess that would've sounded quite a lot to you in those days. Where were you? How did they meet you?'

'On the streets. On the streets hiding from you lot, on the streets trying to keep our nose clean and find some food for the next day. Lo and behold, here comes a job, but it's not nice, but when you got to eat, you have to do it.'

'So those with you, were they from the street as well?' The man went suddenly quiet. 'I asked a question. Were they from the streets as well? Did they bring everybody from the streets?' Again, there was silence. 'If you're all on the streets, I will not know who you are, will I? It's not as if I'm going to… If you want people like this put away, this is not how you do it,' said Macleod. 'You needed to come to us. We needed to investigate.' Macleod leaned in on the desk. 'You need to embrace the law.'

'Embrace the law! Embrace the fucking law!' cried the man. 'Do you know how many people I went to who ignored me? Do you know how often it was covered up? They covered it up in Lewis as well, didn't they? You covered it up.'

The man flung himself forward and nutted Macleod, smacking the forehead, and sending him backward off his chair. It clattered on the ground and Macleod's head spun. The man struggled against his cuffs to break free from the table he was at.

Macleod heard the constable asking if he was okay, but he waved away his attentions although his head was spinning. He needed to get back on the front foot. Macleod dragged himself up sloppily, but at least he was upright and he slammed his fist down on the table.

'I have never covered up anything of the like.'

'You were there. You were there. Donald Anderson, the high and mighty Reverend Donald Anderson. He did it to Malcolm.'

'Well then, where's Malcolm?'

'Malcolm's dead. Malcolm died many years ago. It's what his brother said.'

'Is his brother in the group with you? Is his brother doing this?'

'No, he's not. He couldn't do this. He didn't want to do it, but you better believe me, Macleod, he's happy we're doing it.'

'What did he do?'

'He took Malcolm, and he had Malcolm in his own way, and you covered it up.'

'I arrived about a week before that case. I was still in my initial training. The man that would've looked after that was McNeil.'

'Oh yes, it was McNeil, all right.'

'No, it wasn't. He might be a lot of things, but McNeil would never cover up anything like that. Not when it was to do with children. Not when a minor was involved. Malcolm's brother has got it wrong. He's believed the stories.'

'Liar,' shouted the man, and he threw himself forward, trying to butt Macleod again, but Seoras was wise to it now. He stepped back casually, out of the way.

'We've identified all the people you want to attack. We've got them. The attack on George Pole was prevented, and they haven't got the time to get over to Gramisdale to get a hold of Patricia Henderson. It's over now. You might as well come clean. If you say the right things, you never know, they might let you off. They might not put you away for as long if you tell us how you've done it, what's involved.'

The man sat back down in his seat and laughed. It was a hideous laugh, manic. It just didn't seem to end. What worried Macleod the most about it was it didn't seem put on.

Seoras ended the interview and returned to his office, making himself a cup of coffee and then to sit down and think about what had happened. As he did so, the phone rang.

'Macleod.'

'Sorry. It's Ross. How are you?'

'What are you doing ringing me? You're out of action. You need to be resting.'

'No,' said Ross. 'Not out of action. I've got my laptop.'

'Who brought you that? Why did they bring it?'

'Don't,' said Ross. 'You need me at the moment. I'll

coordinate from here. I'm just going to sit and do nothing otherwise. Besides, the leg's okay. I will not lose anything. They're just making sure there's no infection. I've got some drugs in me taking away the pain. But I am good to work.'

'If I say no, then you're just going to ignore me, anyway. That's the trouble with you three. You always do that. If you want to work, Ross, work, but it's not an order. Make sure you take care of yourself. Make sure you rest up as well. I'm going to need you back at full fitness, not coming back half a mess.'

'Very good, sir.'

Macleod brought him up to speed with everything else that was happening and then told Ross to sit back and relax and said that Sandra Carson was picking up his end.

'I'm putting the phone down.'

He called the hospital arranging for an assessment to take place of Peter Samson. Macleod spent the next twenty minutes organising a car and officers to accompany the man to the interview. He wanted the assessment done quickly to see what information he could gather from him.

Was everyone like this? Were they all broken up and busted? Is that what this was about? A revenge from victims. How had they made the arrangements? Macleod sat back in his chair.

If they could trace through all the victims, surely, they could pull in the entire group. They could sort this unless…A terrible thought struck him.

How many others were there and how were they going to get them? At least if they had the last two ministers in protective custody, they'd be okay. Barclay had been the ringleader of the group, though, and they'd gone for him first.

Macleod glanced across at the card. It still hadn't been picked up by forensics. *Who in their right mind*, he thought, *would want to do that to a person, to enjoy, to experiment? Bizarre.* He sat back, knowing there was just one piece to finish. Clarissa needed to get down and pick up Henderson. He made a call downstairs and Sandra Carson answered.

'I just wanted to check that local uniform got hold of Henderson.'

'No, they didn't. Couldn't find her at the house. They're keeping a lookout.'

Macleod became a little uneasy. He put down the phone and then picked it up again to ring Clarissa.

'Just on the ferry,' she said.

'Good,' said Macleod. 'Get there as quick as you can. I'm not convinced you're going to be on your own when you meet her.'

Chapter 24

Clarissa sped the little green car across North Uist and into Benbecula with a nervous Patterson at her side. She could see the man's hand shaking and wondered just what he thought they were getting into.

'Are you all right?' she asked.

'Ross is down. They were attacked. Hope and Susan both attacked as well. We could be heading into something.'

'It's unlikely. Everybody's over on the mainland. They haven't had time to get over here.'

'No, but the boss is worried. He's worried because they may be here. He thinks there's more people.'

'How many people can you have in something like this?' asked Clarissa. 'We'll get down here, and we'll pick her up. Get her up into custody, up and stored away, somewhere out of reach. You'll see, it'll be fine. Where am I going?'

Patterson pointed out the roads and Clarissa kept him on his toes by racing the car around every corner. The wind was whipping through her hair, and she felt alive, but something from Patterson was ringing in her ears. Was he right? This wasn't her forte, the overview. This way of seeing the big picture wasn't Clarissa.

Her forte was getting stuck in, knocking the truth out of people, realising what was going on by being amongst it. She wasn't one to be reflecting, looking out a window. You found out where the action was happening and you got in there, and then you stirred up enough till the truth got to the surface.

The little green car turned round a large bend to see a house sitting off the road. On the driveway, Clarissa could see a black van. Her heart sank.

'Patterson, is that the house?'

'Yes, it is.'

'Well, call for backup then. Looks like you were right.'

Clarissa drove past the house quickly while Patterson made his call, then turned around and came back. The van hadn't moved.

She drove her little sports car and parked it across the driveway before climbing out.

'Where are we going?' asked Patterson.

'She could be in there and she could be in trouble,' said Clarissa. 'We've called for backup. Let's get in and sort it out.'

'Look, Sarge,' said Patterson, 'no harm to you, but you've got to be a sixty-year-old woman.'

Clarissa turned to him, teeth bared. 'And I've taken down plenty of you whippersnappers. That woman's in trouble, we go help. Now, move it.'

Clarissa didn't run to the door. Rather, she strode, still with her trademark shawl wrapped around her. The wind was strong, as it was so often on the Western Isles. She could also feel a slight drizzle coming in.

As she approached the door, Clarissa pushed it gently and found it locked. The door had a circular glass pane at the top, with a decorative imprint. Clarissa reckoned that if she got her arm through it, she could probably reach down and undo the latch. Without hesitation, she turned onto the driveway, picked up a large boulder, and flung it at the glass.

It smashed, and she reached through quickly, opening the door, but as she did so, she heard footsteps. She could hear a thwack as the sound of a bullwhip reverberated in the air, but in front of her, down the stairs, charged a masked woman in black.

She was petite, possibly a few inches shorter than Clarissa, but she wasn't holding back. Clarissa stepped to the side, caught the woman with her left hand over the face, and drove her down. The feet came out from under the woman, and she fell, hitting her head on the floor below.

Clarissa tore up the stairs the woman had come down. As she reached the top, someone opened a door and raced along the landing towards her. They had a knife and Clarissa tore off her shawl, wrapping it between both hands in front of her. As the man stabbed the knife at her, she closed the shawl around him and then hit him as hard as she could with her hip. He stumbled into the banister, and it gave way. He fell down to the hall below.

Clarissa opened the door in front of her and was greeted with the sight of a naked woman lying on the ground, but before her was a woman dressed in black. She had a mask on, like all of her colleagues. She turned and cracked the whip towards Clarissa. It struck her on the arm and her skin split open, revealing a deep red gash that bled.

'You bitch,' shouted Clarissa and ran at the woman. There was a crack of the whip, but Clarissa knew better than to stop. Somewhere behind her, the whip found a mark on the floor, but it had missed Clarissa, who ran into the woman with her shoulder, taking her to the ground. The woman's head banged off something, and Clarissa fought to get back up.

'Patterson,' she yelled, 'are you okay?'

There came a cry from downstairs, but Clarissa looked over at the naked woman. With an effort, she put two arms underneath her shoulders, pulled her upright before bending down and lifting the woman over her shoulder.

As she turned, the woman with the whip was stirring. Clarissa lunged across the room, with the figure of Patricia Henderson over her shoulder. Clarissa wasn't quick. She had enough speed that when she arrived at the woman in black who was just lifting her head off the floor, she was able to launch a kick into her face before making for the door.

It was time to get out. She ran down the stairs as quickly as she could, desperate not to topple over with the weight on her shoulder. As she reached the lower steps, she found Patterson engaged with another man in black.

He was pushing Patterson back, throttling him. With her spare hand, Clarissa reached forward and jabbed two fingers into the eyes of Patterson's attacker. The man dropped his hands. As someone else ran along the lower hallway, Clarissa could see the struggling figure of a man on the floor, seemingly in desperate pain from his fall from up above.

Beyond him was another woman who jumped at Clarissa, pulling at her hair. Clarissa shrieked. She stumbled backwards, driving Patricia Henderson's body into the wall. She couldn't hold her any longer and the naked woman slipped off her. The area was cramped, making fighting difficult, but Clarissa reached out, found her attacker's ear, and twisted it violently. She then felt her shoulder being bitten into.

215

Desperately, she kicked up with her knees, driving them into the woman's mid-rift. The woman fell off her momentarily and Clarissa reached down again, grabbing hold of Henderson's naked form. Patterson had been driven back onto the stairs by the man, and they were exchanging blows. Clarissa managed to half stumble out of the house before pitching down onto the ground, Henderson tumbling from her shoulders. All she needed to do was get to the car, just get to the car. She saw Patterson step out of the house.

'We're all clear,' he said. 'Let's go!'

Something hit him in the back. He spun, and Clarissa saw the knife. The man in black swiped it and cut across Patterson's throat. He reached up, grabbing his neck before falling to the ground. The man then ran towards Clarissa.

She looked around desperately, saw a gnome on the ground, and picked it up. As the man approached, she threw it from almost point-blank range, catching him smack in the face. He stumbled backwards, and she kicked him hard, first in the knee, then into his groin, before she nutted him. Her breathing was heavy now, and she could hear Patterson struggling on the floor, gurgling. The man she had nutted was coming to his feet.

'You bitch,' he shouted. 'I'll get you for that, you bitch.'

'Come on,' yelled Clarissa. She was beyond her limit now, panting heavily. She'd always been a scrapper, but these days things just felt harder to do.

Clarissa looked up and saw a woman emerging from the house with a man half-hanging around her neck. She was helping him towards the black van. Beyond her, another woman stepped out with a bullwhip and started coming towards Clarissa. This wasn't looking good.

And then sirens split the air.

'Go!' shouted the man, supported by the woman. 'We go. We've got to go. No time, just go.'

The man with the knife ran towards Clarissa, took a lunge that she stepped aside from, and then received a blow with the back of her hand to the rear of his head. He stumbled forward. Clearly, it wasn't as strong a blow as Clarissa had hoped, and the man then ran towards the van.

The woman with the bullwhip cracked it several times, preventing Clarissa from following them. As they jumped into the van, she looked over towards Patterson. He was struggling with his throat. Blood was everywhere. She hauled herself up, ran over to him, and dropped, placing both hands across his windpipe.

'Keep going,' she yelled at him. 'Keep going.' There was an almighty crash, and she looked up to see her sports car being spun off the driveway down into a ditch by the fast-escaping van. It reached the main road and tore off. A police car pulled into the drive towards her.

'Ambulance,' she screamed. 'Ambulance and get after those bastards!' The car turned, raced away, and Clarissa fought to remember her first aid. She had to keep his windpipe connected. She had to keep it sealed. Pack the throat.

She reached inside her pockets, pulling out handkerchiefs, slapping them onto the man's neck. She had to stop the blood. Apply pressure. His lungs were still going. He was still breathing, albeit in fits and spats. She manoeuvred herself around him, lifting him upright, trying to get his throat above the heart.

'Ambulance,' she cried. 'Ambulance!' She looked down at her hand. It was drenched in blood. Her shirt was stained.

Her own arms smarted from the whip. She looked around and could see people in far-off houses. Clarissa screamed loudly.

A woman approached, but it seemed like an age to get to her. Tears were streaming down Clarissa's face as panic set in. Patterson was in her arms. Patterson was dying right before her. As the woman got close, Clarissa screamed at her, 'Ambulance, get a damn ambulance. Make sure there's an ambulance.'

The heavens opened and rain poured down, soaking Clarissa as she held on, keeping as hard a pressure on his throat as she could. She could barely see now because of the rain dripping off her hair onto her face and the tears pouring down.

We'd barely started as a team, she thought. His crisp white shirt was a mess. He'd said not to go. He'd said to wait for backup.

She looked over and saw Patricia Henderson stirring. Clarissa shouted at the woman who had come over from the house to find blankets to deal with Henderson, and then she heard more sirens. There were blue lights and a large white van.

When the paramedics stepped in, she stumbled back, fell onto her backside, and began crying into her hands. They were good with him, so good, and had him whisked away in no time at all. Another neighbour had come across and he put his arms around Clarissa, asking, 'Was she okay?'

She looked at the blood on the ground, Patterson's blood, and her little green car, half smashed, lying in a ditch. 'I can't do this,' she yelled at the man holding her. 'I can't do this no more.'

'It's all right, love,' he said. 'It's okay.'

'No, it bloody isn't,' she said.

A chill went over her. She felt cold and numb. Someone put a blanket around her, tried to get her to stand, and she was led away to someone's house.

Chapter 25

His partner, Jane, was speaking to him on the phone, but Macleod wasn't listening. Jane was simply running through her day, talking about the little odd bits and pieces. When Macleod was on a case, he couldn't speak to her about it. He sat and listened to what she had to say, a reminder that the rest of the world still went on. But today it wasn't. It was all a damn mess.

The bright side was they'd saved two people. Patricia Henderson was certainly not in a great state, but she was alive. George Pole, also known as Steven Jolly, was also alive, and talking about this previous life. He would get help, though Macleod wasn't sure if he deserved it. His emotions were fraught now.

He was angry at Steven Jolly, and the rest of them that had caused the initial problem, who had done such damage to these people. Angry at these people that they felt the need to kill. Livid that Clarissa hadn't got better back up. He was angry that Hope had taken half a beating as well.

But he was truly angry about Ross, for he was there, and that was his fault. He'd rushed in, Clarissa had rushed in, because they were there to save people. People he wasn't even sure if they were worth saving. He didn't mean that, or maybe he did. The good book always talked about redemption for all. Sometimes he wondered if certain people were worth the bother.

Hope had come back with Cunningham, and they were downstairs now, finishing reports. Clarissa would be in shortly. Patterson had been flown away from Benbecula and was stable in the hospital. Clarissa had hung on long enough. They got to him; they'd stabilised him. He'd survive. He'd be okay physically in time.

How he was going to be mentally. Who could tell? Injuries like that in the line of duty often had very negative consequences on the individual's mentality. Macleod hoped it wouldn't be so. His genuine worry was with Clarissa. She'd spoken to him only briefly, and everything had been a shout. Macleod had immediately called Frank Macleod, the groundskeeper that Clarissa was seeing, telling him she needed him. Now she'd arrived back at the airport, and he'd be meeting her shortly.

The little green car looked like it would be a write off. Losing Patterson would have been a much bigger hit. A devastating blow. But Macleod didn't want to underestimate that car, and what it meant to Clarissa. She'd really taken a whammy this time round. She'd been off ever since seeing that body.

There was a knock at his door, to which he said, 'Come in.' His secretary brought Clarissa through. She was in a blue bomber jacket, her tartan shawl having been taken away as evidence from inside the house. She had changed into a set of jeans and a T-shirt, probably the most that they could find for her in Benbecula. At least now she was back. Macleod walked forward to give her a hug, and she stepped away.

'Don't, Seoras, don't. I'm done. I'm bloody done.'

'You did well,' he said. 'You saved him.'

'I sent us in,' she said. 'I sent us in, and he nearly died. Sixty, I'm passing sixty, Seoras. What am I doing? Why am I charging around like this? I need to put my feet up. I need to be…'

'You do it because it's in your blood, because it's you. It's the way you are.'

'Then I need to be somebody else. If those blue lights hadn't have got there, Patterson wouldn't have been the only one dead. Four of them. Four of them, and where did they come from? They were meant to be on the mainland.'

'Clearly, there's more than four,' said Macleod. He thanked the secretary, telling her she could go. When she'd shut the door, Macleod turned to Clarissa. 'You can speak freely now.'

'I held him. Do you get that, Seoras? I held him. Grabbed his windpipe and held him. I had to pack it. Saw him choke. I did that, leaving a naked woman whipped to pieces beside me because I couldn't deal with her as well. I was screaming at a neighbour to get stuff done.'

'You did it, and you saved him.'

'We didn't get any of them,' said Clarissa. 'When does this end?'

'It will end now. It should do,' said Macleod. 'We've got the two they haven't killed. There's no more in the group. It's just the five of them from the university.'

'I'm out,' said Clarissa.

'Take time, think about it. Go home, rest up. I've asked Frank to come in.' There was almost a flicker of encouragement on her face. Then it died.

'No, I should have stuck with Art. I'd have attended gala balls. I'd have been in the finest chateaus, looking at paintings, working with insurance agents. They'd take you for lunch sometimes. Not to the middle of a murder site.'

'Take your time,' said Macleod. 'I need you on this team.'

'I don't care,' said Clarissa. 'No more! Noone can take what I've just taken.'

'You'll recover,' said Macleod. 'You will. There'll be help. You'll get back up.'

She turned on him and slapped him hard across the cheek. 'Seoras, piss off!' She turned on her heel, marched to the door and flung it open, thumping her way down the stairs.

'You can piss off too.'

Obviously, some poor, unsuspecting soul had crossed her on the stairs. Macleod slowly followed down the stairs and found Clarissa at her desk. She was packing things up. He watched as she stared at what normally would have been Ross's desk. She stepped over and touched it and then broke down into tears again. Macleod came over, but she shrugged him off.

'You nearly lost Als. He's a good kid,' she said. 'He's a good kid.'

Hope came out of her office and raced over to Clarissa. She went to put her arms around her, but she shrugged them off again. 'Don't. Don't.'

'You'll be all right in time,' said Hope. 'There are ways and means. These things don't have to turn this way.'

Clarissa turned again. 'You can piss off too,' she said.

'Clarissa, don't. That's not you talking. Don't.'

Macleod looked over to see his namesake, Frank, approaching. Clarissa turned and ran, flinging herself into the man's arms. Her face was a mess, tears everywhere, hair bedraggled. But he didn't care. Frank Macleod took hold of her, held her tight.

'I'm going to get you home,' he said. 'I'm going to get you home, and when you're ready, you can look forward to life with me.'

She stopped, noticed he was on his knee. The rest of the unit froze. He lifted a ring. 'I know it's not the best of times, but I was going to do it when you were done with this case, and you're done.'

She hugged him tight, then took the ring and put it on her finger. Without another word, she walked out of the office. Frank stood up and turned to Macleod.

'I'll look after her. Don't worry. She'll be all right.'

'She's welcome back,' said Macleod. 'Just whenever she's ready.'

'I'm not sure about that.'

Macleod looked up at Hope, but her face was one of anguish. Cunningham looked bemused. Some of the rest of the constables were trying to look away. Macleod didn't know what to say. How could you make a speech now? How could he address them, when they'd seen his Rottweiler, his sergeant, falling apart in front of them? He turned to Hope. She just raised their shoulders.

'I don't know, Seoras. I don't know.'

He turned and trudged away, back up the stairs to his office.

He got little done for the rest of that day. Yes, there were reports. There was talk about where Henderson and Steven Jolly would be to keep them safe. Nobody had been arrested for the killings, and the hunt would continue. They'd have to discover who'd been abused. They'd have to go back to Edinburgh, and dig up historical evidence, but at least, nobody else was going to die. He felt weary.

Sometimes, in cases, he felt that justice was served, but part of him almost thought that the killers getting away with it was a justice of sorts. After all, they had obviously been brutally mistreated by these people. He found it hard to imagine that a ring like that was set up, that for so long it hadn't come out. Why hadn't these people come to him? He thought about Donald Anderson. He thought about the case over there. It couldn't be real. McNeil wouldn't have done that. He wouldn't have shied away.

The trouble with police work was you needed evidence. Not just hearsay, not just coincidence. He'd found his coffee and stood up, and then picked up the mug and threw it off the wall. It shattered, leaving a coffee stain. There was a knock at the door. Lorraine walked in.

'Are you okay, Inspector?'

'It's Seoras,' he said. 'It's flaming Seoras.' Then he caught himself. 'I'm fine, sorry. Don't worry about the wall. I'll clean the wall.'

Macleod remained in his office for the next four hours. It was getting dark, and he was hiding away from everything, brooding on it. He wasn't convinced. He wasn't happy about what had happened. Something was up. Something wasn't correct here.

He looked at the clock. It was three in the morning. Had he been here for four hours? Maybe he'd fallen asleep. Maybe he'd..., whatever. He was going home. Jane wouldn't be worried because she probably thought he was busy. The truth was, he was discombobulated. He didn't know where he was. As he put on his coat, there was a knock at the door.

'Come in,' he said, wondering who would be calling at this hour.

'Seoras, you haven't gone. Good. Sit back down. Ross is

coming.'

'Ross is coming? What do you mean Ross is coming? It's three in the morning.'

'He wouldn't say what's up, but he said he needed your office, and he needed you.'

'Is he okay?'

'Physically, apart from the wound, he's okay. That's going to need to heal up, but it seems he can move about okay.'

'Good,' he said. 'You hear any more from Clarissa?'

'No,' said Hope. 'I thought it best if I leave it. You don't think she's really…?'

'Maybe,' said Macleod. 'Maybe. I spoke to Patterson's wife earlier. She's okay, shocked. I think we'd all be, if somebody took a knife to our loved one. Still, he's going to recover. Hopefully, he'll be all right.'

'Do you want a coffee?'

'Why not? Make one for Ross. He's always punctual.'

Hope made coffee. One for Macleod, one for herself, and one for Ross. She barely put it down on the desk when the door was knocked, and it opened to reveal a limping Ross.

'Three a.m., Ross, what's going on? You should be getting rest.'

Ross walked over slowly, an exaggerated limp, before tossing a book on Macleod's table. 'I got it from Jona. The code book found with Peter Samson. I've cracked it.'

Macleod was flabbergasted but was caught out by his desk phone ringing. He glanced and took it, seeing it was from the hospital. He put his hand up to Ross and answered the phone.

'Hello.'

'Hi, it's PC Martin here. Is that the inspector?'

'This is Seoras Macleod. What can we do for you?'

'I was one of the detail who was sent to the hospital with Peter Samson. I'm afraid, sir, he's dead.'

'Dead? How?'

'We were transferring him from one ward to the other. He got up off the trolley and ran right through the window, five floors up. Just a mess. Only words were "My part is complete". He was manic.'

'We'll be down,' said Macleod. He placed the phone down and looked up at Hope. 'Peter Samson is dead. He committed suicide. They said he left manically, told them, "My part is complete."'

'That's what I was trying to say to you, sir, before that phone call. This is a codebook, and from what I can decipher, this group may be over fifty strong. There's more out there, sir. There's more coming, but I just don't know from where.'

'We better get started,' said Macleod. He watched Ross turn, and Hope, and they both exited the room. Macleod took his coat and his hat, and he stopped for a moment.

Clarissa is out. Patterson's out. It's time to knuckle down, he thought. *Time we got a proper success.* He walked over to his door, stepped out, closed it, and locked it. There was more to come.

Read on to discover the Patrick
Smythe series!

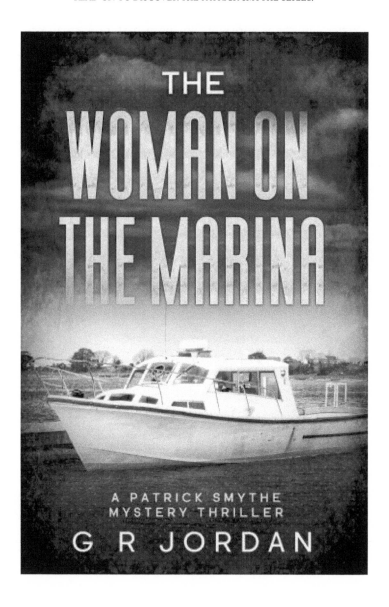

THE
WOMAN ON THE MARINA

A PATRICK SMYTHE
MYSTERY THRILLER

G R JORDAN

Patrick Smythe is a former Northern Irish policeman who after suffering an amputation after a bomb blast, takes to the sea between the west coast of Scotland and his homeland to ply his trade as a private investigator. Join Paddy as he tries to work to his own ethics while knowing how to bend the rules he once enforced. Working from his beloved motorboat 'Craigantlet', Paddy decides to rescue a drug mule in this short story from the pen of G R Jordan.

Join G R Jordan's monthly newsletter about forthcoming releases and special writings for his tribe of avid readers and then receive your free Patrick Smythe short story.

Go to https://bit.ly/PatrickSmythe for your Patrick Smythe journey to start!

About the Author

GR Jordan is a self-published author who finally decided at forty that in order to have an enjoyable lifestyle, his creative beast within would have to be unleashed. His books mirror that conflict in life where acts of decency contend with self-promotion, goodness stares in horror at evil, and kindness blindsides us when we at our worst. Corrupting our world with his parade of wondrous and horrific characters, he highlights everyday tensions with fresh eyes whilst taking his methodical, intelligent mainstays on a roller-coaster ride of dilemmas, all the while suffering the banter of their provocative sidekicks.

A graduate of Loughborough University where he masqueraded as a chemical engineer but ultimately played American football, Gary had worked at changing the shape of cereal flakes and pulled a pallet truck for a living. Watching vegetables freeze at -40'C was another career highlight and he was also one of the Scottish Highlands "blind" air traffic controllers. These days he has graduated to answering a telephone to people in trouble before telephoning other people to sort it out.

Having flirted with most places in the UK, he is now based in the Isle of Lewis in Scotland where his free time is spent between raising a young family with his wife, writing, figuring out how to work a loom and caring for a small flock of chickens. Luckily, his writing is influenced by his varied work and life experience as the chickens have not been the poetical inspiration he had hoped for!

You can connect with me on:

🌐 https://grjordan.com

f https://facebook.com/carpetlessleprechaun

Subscribe to my newsletter:

✉ https://bit.ly/PatrickSmythe

Also by G R Jordan

G R Jordan writes across multiple genres including crime, dark and action adventure fantasy, feel good fantasy, mystery thriller and horror fantasy. Below is a selection of his work. Whilst all books are available across online stores, signed copies are available at his personal shop.

The Guilty Parties (Highlands & Islands Detective Book 27)
https://grjordan.com/product/the-guilty-parties
Cryptic clues beyond the newspaper crossword. Old cases that were pushed aside for all the wrong reasons. Will Macleod and McGrath prevail as the Avenging Angel seeks out larger conspiracies?

Angry at the escape of the serial killers they pursued across Scotland, DCI Macleod and DI McGrath are assigned to the deaths of prominent business leaders at a conference. When evidence points to the return of the black clad group, the pair must go on a nationwide man-hunt before they strike again at the heart of the financial sector.

Sometimes, we must all take the blame.

Infiltrator (A Kirsten Stewart Thriller #10)

https://grjordan.com/product/infiltrator

Secrets being leaked from an overseas embassy. A mole too clever to be fooled by standard red herrings. Can Kirsten keep herself alive and find the mole before he discovers her cover?

Back in the pay of the British secret services, Kirsten must travel to South America where secrets are being passed through a mole known only as 'The Goldsmith'. But as Kirsten unearths the true nature of the information being passed, she finds herself in a race against time to stop a dirty bomb that goes right for the heart of British society.

The countdown has begun!

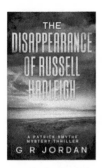

The Disappearance of Russell Hadleigh (Patrick Smythe Book 1)
https://grjordan.com/product/the-disappearance-of-russell-hadleigh
A retired judge fails to meet his golf partner. His wife calls for help while running a fantasy play ring. When Russians start co-opting into a fairly-traded clothing brand, can Paddy untangle the strands before the bodies start littering the golf course?

In his first full novel, Patrick Smythe, the single-armed former policeman, must infiltrate the golfing social scene to discover the fate of his client's husband. Assisted by a young starlet of the greens, Paddy tries to understand just who bears a grudge and who likes to play in the rough, culminating in a high stakes showdown where lives are hanging by the reaction of a moment. If you love pacey action, suspicious motives and devious characters, then Paddy Smythe operates amongst your kind of people.

Love is a matter of taste but money always demands more of its suitor.